crossing over

CLEMSON
LITERATURE
SERIES
CONVERSE

As a partnership between Clemson University Press and the Converse College Low Residency MFA program, this series publishes poetry collections, short-story collections, and creative nonfiction.

crossing over

kim shegog

ISBN 978-1-63804-032-3

Published by Clemson University Press.
Visit our website to learn more about our publishing program:
www.clemson.edu/press.

Typeset by Kirstin O'Keefe with the assistance of Emily Rose Campbell, Caroline Cardoso, Sadie Chafe, Liam Conley, Alex Crume, Mary Dixon, Whitney Edgerly, Tyrell Fleshman, Jordan Green, Emma Hammel, AnnaRae Hammes, Olivia Hanline, Anna Higgins, Mary Frances Huggins, Cece Lesesne, Bucky O'Malley, Michael Ondrus, Clarence Orr, Kathryn Rabon, Fran Smith, and Jordan Thurman.

For Eli and Samuel

Speak, for your servant is listening.

1 Sam. 3:10

Contents

Crossing Over

Family is a fine thing until people get in the way. Patty, surprised by her revelation, explored each face trapped at the table, a web of young and old and greats and grands, all with faces reddened by hot dishes or hot liquor or both. Fools and drunks, including some of the women, and one or two maybe worse, but a little bit of each flowed through her veins. They could be kind or even captivating, a thought she liked to keep in her mind. Patty's father was one of these, flawed but forgivable at times. It helped that his dark chestnut-colored eyes and matching hair made him handsome. A fact she knew because one of her girlfriends had told her so.

"Mama's the one named me Georgia," he said, raising his cleft chin. "Took me two years, but I earned it. Virgil and Louis—they never made it past their first birthdays. When me and Mother and Papa made it over the Tennessee line in 1925, she slapped me on the back and claimed I was her Georgia boy."

The only thing he did well when he was drinking was tell a story, and there was no better time to tell a story than at the dinner table on Thanksgiving when there was nowhere to go even if somebody wanted to.

They'd all heard Georgia's story before, many times. He told it every year, but they laughed and slapped the table in between mouthfuls of fried apples and cornbread dressing. Patty laughed hardest. It was a treat for the fifteen-year-old to observe her father acting like anyone else's father for a little while. Her mother, too, was normal. She sat with a shy grin, smiling as the crowd gorged themselves on her dishes, her craft glorified through bulging cheeks and grinding teeth.

Like most of her girlfriends' parents, Patty's mother and father met at church, though their meeting had been a little different than most. Her mother'd caught him smoking in the garden shed by the cemetery. After church, she'd walked through the grass, weaving in between the gravestones, waiting for her mother to finish chatting with the ladies about hats and gloves and such. She found him reclined on the cement floor, his back propped against a few canvas sacks. He offered her a cigarette, a non-filter, her first of any kind, and they sat in the shed, trapped in silver smoke and infatuation. They married the next year when she was supposed to be a junior in high school, but she quit. Georgia told her schooling didn't matter anyway. He'd only made it through the sixth grade, and he had a good position on the assembly line at the carpet plant.

Grandma Ruth sat across the table from Patty. Patty stared, moved her gaze to her mother and then back to her grandmother. These two women shared nothing, she confirmed. Grandma Ruth was a good deal smaller than Patty's mother, and her face, blessed with high, tight cheekbones, made Patty think of Artemis, or any one of those beautiful Greek goddesses she'd read about in school. Her scent, a perfume blend of cloves and cut strawberries, radiated a feminine warmth around her. Patty didn't think of anyone else when she looked at her mother. Hair in a bun. Curved shoulders. Apron strings in a knot. Scuffed heels. Always, only, a mother.

Besides her beauty, Grandma Ruth had worked. Not like Patty's mother with her simple cooking and cleaning and washing. She'd worked at a manufacturing job in Dalton, helping to design embroidery patterns for quilts, grand peacocks and lily flowers her specialties. She still kept her design booklets in the cedar chest at the foot of her bed. Patty'd found them a few years earlier while spending the night. She'd asked her grandmother to show her pictures of her grandfather before he'd lost his good sense and run off.

"You're an artist," Patty said to her grandmother after listening to her share part of her history. "A real, live artist and my grandma, too."

To compensate for her embarrassment, Grandma Ruth had buried the pattern book under her red fox stole and brass photo frames. After closing the lid without a word, she had climbed into bed in her housecoat.

"Patty. Did you hear your Uncle Billy?" her mother asked, wiping her thin lips with her clean cloth napkin. "He's talking to you."

Patty turned her head toward her uncle. No matter her response, it'd be the wrong thing. After all, what did children know? A statement he'd made before.

The truth was Uncle Billy was jealous of his older brother, Georgia. For Patty, it was plain to see. Uncle Billy was as round as a tire on a school bus and bald besides. He did make a pile of money somewhere though, and the money earned him a parade of lady friends, some from another state. "Couldn't decide which one should have the pleasure," he'd explained when Georgia asked him where his date was for supper. Last year, it was Rose from Nashville who swore her cousin knew Johnny Cash. Patty and her father shared a love for the country singer, sometimes singing a duet to "Don't Take Your Guns to Town," when it came on the radio in the Pontiac.

"Don't bother her, brother," Georgia said, slapping Billy on the back. "She's always thinking about one thing or another. Half the time she don't know what's real and what's not," Georgia said, downing the last bit of bourbon in his glass.

His audience grinned like Sunday ushers with the collection plates, nodding in approval of his contribution.

Patty's cheeks spiked red. She turned an apple slice on its side with her fork, gauging it into several pieces. She knew more than they gave her credit for.

First, she knew most husbands and wives loved each other. She knew because she saw it on television, re-runs of *The Donna Reed Show* for one. And one night when she'd joined her friend Kay for supper, she saw Kay's father pull out the chair for his wife. Then Patty was bringing the dirty dishes into the kitchen, and she saw him rubbing her shoulders. Patty couldn't remember seeing her parents do anything of the sort. The closest they came was on a Sunday, years ago, and they were all in the living room reading the newspaper. Patty sat on the floor with the funnies while her mother and father sat on opposite ends of the couch. Patty's mother asked for the obituaries, which Georgia passed to her. When she took hold of the paper, her fingers brushed the back of his hand, and she kept them there longer than was necessary. His cheeks turned red, like Patty's often did, his shoulders relaxed, and he was satisfied for a moment.

Second, she knew fathers weren't supposed to drink as much as hers although it did help liven things up sometimes, and she knew mothers, for the most part, liked having daughters, that they should do things together, like go to church, and they should have picnics on the weekends in warm weather like some of her friends' families. It shouldn't be Grandma Ruth taking Patty to church. The four of them should be going together. It'd be better if her parents argued, raised their voices at one another, anything instead of what they did in silence: him going to work and coming home, sometimes working on the furnace or mowing the yard, her getting up the breakfast dishes and hanging the clothes on the line, once in a while asking Patty how her day was at school. Patty's home was a ghost town out of a Western.

"Georgia, don't tease her so," Grandma Ruth said, patting his shoulder. "She's just a young thing." Even Grandma Ruth, Patty's favorite, believed her to be a child, all ignorance and misunderstanding.

"Everybody eat up." Patty's mother passed the bowl of snap beans to Grandma Ruth, who took none, sitting the bowl on the table.

"You've outdone yourself again," Uncle Billy said, picking up the bowl. "Georgia, I tell you, you are a lucky man." He poured a heaping spoonful of beans onto his plate.

"Don't I know it. Lucky from the beginning to have such a fine wife."

"Mother, your biscuits are perfect," Patty's mother said, breaking one open, placing the two halves on her plate. "I never could get mine to taste like yours."

"I didn't cook. You know that," said Grandma Ruth. "The one thing I did well was those biscuits. I thought I'd shown you what to do. I know Patty and I made them together before. She can teach you. Surely she remembers."

"I might have her do that," Patty's mother said, spinning the two halves with her fork.

"Patty baked biscuits?" Georgia asked, reaching for the gravy boat. "I heard you tell one of your little friends how you'd never be like your mama, wasting her time in the kitchen."

Again, Patty's cheeks burned. If she'd keep her eyes low and focused on her plate, nobody'd notice. She did say that but only to Kay. They'd been riding their bicycles up the driveway when she'd told her she wanted to be a nurse and not waste her time in the kitchen like her mother. Kay argued with her. She told her how she'd be happy as a lark if she were married with a couple of children, a boy and a girl, and cooking was how a mother showed her love, and love was hard work. Her mother'd told her so. Patty called her crazy, and they pedaled to the store for peanut butter cups and magazines.

"She'll learn," Uncle Billy said, shaking his finger at Patty. "She'll grow out of selfish sooner than she thinks."

They continued gorging themselves at the feast, grabbing for one more drop biscuit and gulping spiced cider, except Grandma Ruth and Patty's mother. Each only nibbled at the food on their plates. Patty's mother preferred to see her guests enjoy their meals, but Grandma Ruth, who, on a regular basis, ate two mayonnaise and tomato sandwiches and a sleeve of saltines for lunch, ate close to nothing.

As the dinner progressed, somebody noticed the window and the heavy flakes of snow on the outside, enough to spread panic among the crowd as one had walked over and one didn't have very good tires while another didn't see well at night anyway. Deep snow never fell in the foothills, especially not in November, so when even the smallest flakes appeared, people grew serious.

They bustled around the table checking dishes to be sure they'd found their owners, packing them and other leftovers in baskets and paper sacks. There were half hugs and almost kisses as they slung coats over their shoulders and shoved hats onto their heads.

Patty closed the front door after they all left and returned to the dining room to find her father and Grandma Ruth relaxed at the table. Her mother, scraping her uneaten biscuit into the garbage, watched them.

"Get your grandma's dishes together, Patty," her mother said, depositing her plate in the sink. "I'm going to walk her home."

It was a good idea, Patty thought. Although Grandma Ruth lived next door, the gravel driveway connecting both the houses might be slick if the snow was sticking.

"I'll walk her home," Georgia said, gripping the table's edge and pushing himself backward.

He didn't stand, only crossed one leg over the other, and smoothed his hair with his hand. Patty's mother clenched her teeth, moving back to her station at the sink.

No one dared challenge Patty's father. The sheriff's deputy couldn't make him follow the rules. When he ran his Pontiac off the road after leaving Ricky's Grill last summer, the deputy tried to take his car keys. He was going to drive him home, but Georgia insisted he was capable, refusing to give the deputy the key. The deputy followed him home to be sure. From her bedroom window, Patty watched the patrolman and her father talk for a moment, and the officer slapped her father on the back, laughed and left. Georgia could be charming.

Patty packed her grandmother's two serving bowls into a small box. Her mother insisted on washing them since she'd borrowed them to hold the cranberries and fresh butter, but Grandma Ruth refused, saying she'd take care of the cleaning later on. Patty looked at her grandmother sitting and talking to her father. A woman who wasn't old but wasn't young either. This woman existed somewhere in the middle.

Patty handed the box to her father, the three of them now by the door. Grandma Ruth pulled on her overcoat and moved toward her granddaughter. She kissed her cheek.

"Sleep well, Mother," Patty's mother called from the kitchen. Her voice drowned in the running water.

Grandma Ruth, turning her head, smiled toward the kitchen and mouthed the words, "I love you."

Patty watched the couple step off the porch into the night.

Her mother was still in the kitchen, cleaning and tidying. She'd scraped all of her leftovers into packages and stored them in the refrigerator. She was standing by the sink drying the dishes when Patty entered.

"Help me put these away," her mother said, irritated. "I can't sleep if the kitchen isn't clear." She kept her attention focused on the glass in her hand, erasing each water droplet. The dishes were stacked in tight rows on the counter waiting to be returned to their resting places.

Patty wished she knew the words to say to start a conversation like the ones the mothers and daughters had on the TV shows when they did the dishes together.

"You're the best," Patty'd say with a broad, toothy grin.

"Dear, it's *my* pleasure. You and your father mean the world to me," her mother'd say in return, gliding across the kitchen to pinch Patty's cheek. "Next week I want you to show me how to make those biscuits. It'll be just you and me in the kitchen, baking and talking. Won't we have the best time?"

It'd be like that if they'd crossed over into television land.

Patty made it through the plates, bowls, and silverware, returning each to its proper resting place. The whole time neither of them spoke a word. Besides not being like the television mothers, she wasn't a good storyteller either. Patty couldn't think of a time when her mother told a story. The closest she came was sharing part of one of her recipes with a lady at church. The woman asked her at a fellowship supper how she made her apple cobbler. Patty noticed she shared all of the ingredients she used except for nutmeg. She'd always used nutmeg in the recipe, so Patty wondered how she forgot to mention it.

Patty put the last glass in the cabinet while her mother was in the dining room brushing the crumbs from the table.

"Darn it," her mother said, loud enough for Patty to hear. She returned to the kitchen holding a pewter breadbasket. "Run this up to Mother's. She'll be sick tonight if she doesn't know where it is." Patty thought her words came too fast like she didn't even know what she was saying. This could wait, but it wouldn't, not for Patty's mother.

Patty took the basket from her mother, waiting until she was by the front door to roll her eyes. She borrowed her father's work shirt from the coatrack, the heavy denim one where her mother had stitched "George" on the pocket. His first day on the job at the plant, another tough guy called him a "sissy," and, Georgia, being young and impatient, split the man's lip. The foreman told him to change his name or his temper, so Patty's mother stitched a tight black *e* at the end of his real name.

Her mother's gardening galoshes sat on the porch, so she pulled those on over her stockings. She looked at her reflection in the storm door. Half of each to make a whole somebody else.

The snow had stopped falling, but the air was still biting cold. There were no sounds except for short gusts of wind spreading through the pine trees, and the pleasant sound of her mother's boots crushing into the gravel beneath her feet. The crest of the Blue Ridge, dissolving into the charcoal sky, reminded Patty of a dream. Relaxed, she searched for the man in the full white moon.

Grandma Ruth's back porch light was on. Patty tapped the screen softly before she opened it. She thought nothing of going inside. She came and went at her grandmother's more than she did her own house. She liked the calm of her grandmother's house. It was peaceful, not the deafening silence common in her home.

Before she'd grown too old, Patty'd visit Grandma Ruth for her regular cosmetic session on Saturdays when her grandmother returned from having her hair set. She'd drag a kitchen chair into the bedroom, planting it opposite her grandmother's stool with the white velvet cushion and brass legs. Grandma Ruth's vanity table was stocked with creams, powders, and liners for various parts of the face. She'd massage thick white lotion onto Patty's face: "good for the skin," and apply a tinted powder with a small puff: "to even a splotchy complexion," curving it with her index finger when working around her eyes. With a rich black pencil, she sketched dark lines at the base of her eyelashes: "men can't resist beautiful eyes." A peach colored rouge cream came next: "Too bad you have your mother's cheeks," followed by a soft coral lipstick: "You're lucky to have a heart-shaped mouth like mine."

Also when Patty was younger, she'd join her grandmother at her house for soap operas, or "stories" as Grandma Ruth called them. She'd jump off the school bus, run up her grandmother's cement walkway, and burst through the front door. She and Grandma Ruth would sit on the green sofa, enjoying spoonfuls of peanut butter right out of the glass jar. All the ladies were beautiful and sophisticated, and the men were handsome in their suits and ties. Sometimes Patty didn't understand why the women cried or the men slammed doors, but she never asked, not wanting to interrupt her grandmother's intense gaze.

The screen door led into a small hallway, containing a bathroom on the side. Patty felt the wall for the light switch, but she couldn't find it just then. She remembered when this part of the house was added on. She was about seven or eight when the men came to build her grandmother a bathroom inside the house. Before, her grandmother used what she called a Johnny-house out back. Patty and her cousin from Virginia made it into a hideout until somebody tore it down.

Now when visitors came to see Grandma Ruth, they came in through the back screen door and not up the cement walkway to the oak front door with the brass doorknocker. Though she said she loved having the indoor bathroom, it was a shame people stopped parking on the streets anymore, preferring to come in through the back door. She wasn't the only one this happened to. She and her lady friends discussed their renovations at church, before and after the service.

Grandma Ruth's bedroom was to the left off of the hallway. Patty figured she might already be asleep, so she'd be quiet. She'd leave the basket so her grandma needn't worry. It'd belonged to her mother, Patty's great-grandmother, a woman known for her ability to give birth to twelve children and have ten of them live. She could also pick pecans like any man, and with a baby strapped to her chest.

Her father was probably long gone by now. He'd come home around the back of their house, through the basement like he often did, especially after he'd been drinking. The basement steps led him up to the kitchen where she'd heard him burst through the door once. She'd cracked her bedroom door to see, and he caught her looking. He was leaning against the wall, and when he saw the light from her table lamp, he laughed and put his finger over his lips.

Patty intended to set the breadbasket on the stovetop and sneak out right quick so as not to wake her grandmother, but when she turned the corner, two shadows caught her eyes.

A large figure lay on top of her grandmother in the bed. It breathed heavy over her face. The bright white moonlight coming through the kitchen window defined the tattoo on the man's shoulder as the couple, wrapped together in the sheets, turned toward her. Patty saw her grandmother's fingertips brush the black wings of the eagle. She recognized the ink immediately. Her father had gotten the tattoo in France during the war, another one of the good stories he told after he'd drunk too much and smoked and drank some more.

Patty took a small step backward, scuffing her boot against the doorjamb. Georgia looked toward the sound and found his daughter, then folded himself back into the room's darkness.

He'd seen her and she'd seen them. With her hand still gripping the breadbasket, Patty turned and with a couple of leaps, she was out the door.

Her heart pounded thick in her chest, its fury rising. She wanted to swallow, clear the offense from her throat, but the bitter cold prevented her attempt. She shuffled through the gravel almost sliding into a hard fall, but catching herself just in time. Running onto the porch, she caught her reflection again in the glass, but did not stop for further inspection. She sat the breadbasket on the concrete step, and removed her mother's boots, placing them gently on the edge of the porch. She opened the screen and turned the doorknob with precision.

The living room was dark except for the flickering light of the color television. They'd been the first family among her friends to own one, a fact she'd bragged about before discovering the awkwardness of being different.

Her mother sat in the center of the couch, her fingers dangling the nub of a lit cigarette over the armrest.

Patty yanked at her father's shirt, pulling and tugging to rid herself from it, her hands shaking as if she'd borrowed them from somebody else, and she couldn't get them to behave for her. She hung the shirt back on its hook making sure his embroidered name faced outward. She wanted her father to see his name, be reminded of all that came with it. Georgia the liar. Georgia the survivor.

Her whole body felt like it was on fire. Every inch of her flesh was burning up. Her stomach rumbled, a chaos of food and nerves and God only knew what else. She swallowed hard like she might throw up or cry. She thought about running out of the door, but there was nowhere for her to go, nowhere for her to be other than where she was right now.

She thought about not saying a word, simply telling her mother goodnight, never looking at her face, and going to bed. She was still young enough to play pretend with all of them. She pictured herself years from now coming home to visit, to celebrate another Thanksgiving, and sitting at the table with her father across from her. He'd wink his handsome eye at her, and she'd want to slap him, but they'd have something between them, a secret nobody else knew, and in some way she couldn't fully understand, it might be what kept them close.

But those thoughts escaped as quickly as they'd entered. She felt a sting inside her heart, maybe in her guts even, something telling her that her mother was worthy of the truth.

"Mama," she said, turning to face her mother. "Mama, Grandma and Daddy, they were—"

"It's fine, Patty." She took a final puff from her cigarette, smashing its face into her brass ashtray. "Come sit by me." She began loosening her hairpins, removing them one by one and collecting them in her palm before pouring them into a mound on the end table.

Patty's mother never rolled her hair in curlers, wrapping her head in a scarf, like the other mothers. She never used a silver brush, only a fine-tooth comb to clear a wet tangle or to help pull back stray hairs when shaping the roll at the nape of her neck, a roll secured by twenty brown bobby pins, hooked into her hair at various angles, each one performing its singular duty. Once a month, she visited Laverne's Beauty Box for a trim, each time enduring Laverne's campaign to improve her looks.

Patty sat next to her mother, her back pressed against the brown cushion, her sock feet flat on the floor. She looked at her mother's light brown hair, the natural curls at the end, hanging over her shoulders. Her fleshy cheeks were flushed in a vibrant red, the color of a ruby ring Patty'd seen once in a department store window. Without the apron, her pale blue dress flattered her chest and shoulders. She sat in her bare feet, her long toes a perfect shade of pink.

"Now we know for sure," she said, her voice firm. She squeezed Patty's hand, her own trembling.

Patty melted into the couch cushions, sliding almost into the floor. Her mind and body flashed over in anger, in disbelief. Her mother'd known all along, or at least suspected, and she'd used her own daughter as a spy.

"I'd thought it for some time," her mother said.

"How could you? I mean why did I have to—" Patty said, taking back her hand from her mother's grip.

Her mother exhaled, lowered her head, and slid her body down, her shoulders now level with her daughter's.

Patty turned toward her mother, examining her profile. Sometimes there wasn't any other way than what people thought best.

She'd be hurt for a long time after tonight, but she was no longer as angry. Now she and her mother, two women, shared their own secret.

Patty's mother, responding to the pressure of her daughter's stare, faced her. Patty saw her cool blue eyes filling with tears. For the first time, Patty believed Frances Hunt Campbell, her mother, was beautiful. In her sadness, she was glowing.

Glory

It was Dimple the yellow rattler got that year. The service had just started getting right with the Lord when he lifted the snake out of the box. He held the rattler up to his forehead like a cool cloth to a fever. Everybody was shouting and praising and stomping their feet telling the Lord to come in and Satan to get out.

That rattler took its thick head and slid right down over Dimple's ear and got him square on the earlobe. It was a while before we knew he'd got bit because he just kept right on holding that snake to his head like it was medicine. Finally, he lifted the snake into his arms like a mama cradling her new baby and laid it back into the box. Then he sat down on the floor up close to the front of the church.

The men and women and even a couple children come rushing around Dimple, praying and crying and singing and rocking back and forth. After a while, some of those little ones curled up on the pew cushions to sleep, their bodies and faith exhausted in the warmth of the night. Even I was envious of their rest.

Dimple died on that floor sometime the next morning though nobody knows exactly when because they was praying and dancing and sweating around him in a holy passion 'til well after the sun had come up.

Folks came from two towns over to his funeral. The pews inside the Temple filled up right quick, and everybody else stood up alongside the windows or at the door. Just about everybody knew Dimple and wanted to pay their respects, though there was probably a few visiting just out of plain curiosity. It had been a long time since one of us had been called on home through a bite though I'd been mighty close a few times.

It was something seeing Dimple lying in that casket. He was dressed in his regular clothes—white collared shirt and brown slacks, and his hair was parted to the left. His face and ears, even the ear that had got bit, and his hands were just as smooth and peach-colored as they all could be. We reasoned that if anybody was deserving of getting his new body sooner rather than later, it was Dimple.

Tom Randall, a member at the Temple, delivered a good service though he could have been a little bit louder. It was right hard to hear him over the women flapping their fans. Eliza, Dimple's wife, was in the front pew. She sat straight up the whole time. Even when Tom offered the closing prayer, she kept her eyes right on Dimple, but I couldn't hardly take a look.

After that, everybody said Dimple was "sorely missed," and he was. Dimple was just the nicest, most soft-spoken man one could ever run into. He used to work at the Feed and Grain where he could lift and stack and haul faster than any other man around. He always had a stick of black licorice in his pocket for the children that walked by there on their way home from school. The services at Meadows Temple just weren't the same after he was gone.

A few weeks after he was buried, a young fellow came up from the college. It was a Wednesday night service, and we just had offered the closing hymn when we heard the door. He walked right down the aisle and up the front with a satchel hanging on his side and pencil behind his ear. A goose feather could've knocked Tom Randall over when he saw that young man walking toward him. We decided this fellow didn't know any better.

"Ladies and gentleman please excuse my interruption. I had knocked on the door, but I suppose no one had heard me," he said. He was tall and thin and wore a yellow sweater that let his white collar peek through. His brown leather shoes shined like copper pennies. He looked straight at us while he talked.

"Richard Wells is my name, and I've come in hopes you will allow me to interview you. The town and the college are very interested in the recent death of your member, Mr. Dimple," he said.

He went on to say something about how he was doing some studying on the subject of snakes and religion and writing an article about it all for the college. He'd come across Dimple's obituary and how he'd passed on during a service. He told us most people couldn't follow exactly what serpent handlers did and why, and he was going to try to enlighten people on the subject.

He moved toward two ladies, one of them Eliza, but they turned their backs to him and stood by the window. When he walked to the other side, a few men waved him off and fussed at some of the children who'd grabbed ahold of the young man's legs. Mr. Wells looked around the sanctuary, but no eyes met his. After a minute, he put his hands in his pockets, half-smiled, and left.

When we couldn't hear his feet in the gravel anymore, a thunderstorm of voices filled the Temple. Some said "He's the Devil" coming in here like that wanting to make a spectacle of Dimple while some believed he "sounded honest" but he could be the "wolf in sheep's clothing." Everybody said the whole event just wasn't "normal." We all agreed right then and there not to talk to him.

That next morning I seen him walking up the road, kicking up the dust on those shiny shoes. Before I could catch myself, I whistled for him and threw up my hand. Reminded me of my younger brother—what he might've looked like had he grown up. Like my brother, this young man had courage. After all, he was still here looking for his answers. He walked up through the front yard and followed me around to the back where we took a seat at the old picnic table under the shed.

"I presume you are a member at the Meadows Temple. Is that correct?" His voice wasn't cold exactly, but there weren't too much warmth in it neither—like hearing the news report on the radio where you can't reconcile the voice with a body.

"It is."

"I have a few questions for you if you don't mind." He opened his satchel, took out a yellow writing tablet, and pulled the pencil from over his ear. "Please state your name."

"Clifton." He lifted his head, wanting more I know, but Clifton was plenty for now.

"Sir, I understand Mr. Dimple didn't receive medical attention after the attack. Could you tell me why?"

"What for?" I asked him right back. "It was God's doing what had been done, and no doctoring could take it out of the hands of the Lord." He shook his head a little when I said that.

"Do you believe your congregation was testing God in that service?" he asked.

"It's faith in the Lord and his plan, nothing more than that," I said. "It was Dimple's desire to hold that yellow rattler up to the Lord in praise. And, that weren't the first time he'd been bit. His hands were scarred up and his fingers looked like roots all twisted up. But that was the time the Lord chose to call him on home."

I told him about the service before the bite. How blind Mrs. Randall stood up and turned around in a circle with her hands raised up while her husband moved around with her, keeping his hand on her shoulder every minute, and how warm it was in the building as the sun was just setting and the soft light was pouring in the windows. I don't know if he was wanting to hear all that the way his foot tapped the ground, but he didn't stop me, and he didn't stop writing on his tablet neither.

I believe I stood up when I was telling him about Miss Esther and Mr. Jim playing their tambourines. It was like I was right back inside that little white building listening to those praises.

"It was a shame the pews weren't even filled up that evening. It was only the Morgans and the Randalls and me there. The Morgans, Ester and Jim, never did have no children, but the Randalls had their three boys with them," I told him. "Too bad Eliza, Dimple's wife, weren't there to be with him, but she was visiting a sister that took sick in Bluefield. Suffered greatly over that we all said. Because she weren't there to hold on to him as he went," I said.

After that, he said he appreciated me taking the time to talk to him, and he needed to get back to his room at the motel to rewrite his notes while everything was still fresh in his mind.

He asked me if I'd mind meeting him tomorrow. He had a few more questions for his report.

When I looked at the tiny beads of sweat on his forehead and the way his eyes squinted at me, I couldn't help myself. I agreed to see him again and talk to him if he was willing to listen.

He came around ten in the morning. His shoes had been shined up fresh but his shirt was wrinkled, and he needed a shave. He had tired eyes, puffed up underneath like he didn't get a good night's rest, but he didn't mention it, and I didn't ask. We went on back to the picnic table and took a seat. My Bible was waiting for us. I offered it to him. He flipped through the pages with his thumb like his was looking for something, and then handed it back to me. He didn't say nothing, so I did.

"And these signs shall follow them that believe; In my name shall they cast out devils; they shall speak with new tongues; They shall take up serpents; and if they drink any deadly thing, it shall not hurt them; they shall lay hands on the sick, and they shall recover," I said. Right there inside was the word of God, telling us what to do so we'd be known as believers.

I heard that young man take a hard swallow, straighten his back, and write something down right quick.

"Well, sir. Do you recall the first time you saw Mr. Dimple handle a serpent?" he asked.

I know I had a smile come across my whole face when he said that 'cause I could feel it. I was sure glad he asked me about that.

"Lord, yes. It was seeing him and his peace that night that changed my heart. Me and Mama had just moved to town. Mama had been asking if there was a good God-fearing church close by that taught the scripture. I believe it was the man from the post office that told her about Meadows Temple. It was a Wednesday evening, and I think I was about thirteen when I first saw Dimple and some other fellas letting them snakes lay real gentle-like on their fingertips and weave in out of their fingers. The folks around them were swaying and singing,

Are you fully trusting in His grace this hour?

Are you washed in the blood of the Lamb?

And when I heard the words, my heart about leapt out my chest and I got the chills from my feet to my ears. Tears started running down my face. I finally got the Spirit. I knew it. When Mama looked down on me, she lifted her hands up to the Lord and closed her eyes and cried like I never seen before. I never did forget how peaceful and pretty she looked that evening."

It's hard to imagine what the fellow wrote on his tablet about all that.

When it got to lunchtime, I asked the fellow if he'd like a sandwich or a cookie. He never took anything more than a drink of water from the spigot on the pump house.

"Sir, how would you respond to the people who believe the members of the Meadows Temple are simple?" he said, keeping his eyes on his tablet.

"I'd say that was just fine for them to think we were simple 'cause we are. Everything we do is in the name of Jesus, so I reckon we should be simple. We have plain clothes and cars and homes because that's all we need. Anything else is a sin and a waste. That's how Mama always put it," I said.

He looked at me kind of strange when I said that, and he didn't write any of it down. At least I don't think he did. He'd cracked his mouth like he wanted to ask me something, but he didn't. Instead, he flipped the page on his tablet and stared it over.

Then he wanted to talk about the snakes. He asked me if I done it. I told him I didn't do it regular, but every once in a while I'd get the feeling. Ever since that first service with Mama I always wondered what them snakes was thinking when they were being held by all them righteous hands. When they stuck them forked tongues out did they know they was tasting holy air—that they was in the Lord's house and the Lamb had conquered the serpent? I told the young man that the reason most of them stayed right calm was because I was pretty sure they knew where they was. It was only when they couldn't take that holiness a minute longer that they did the only thing they could, and that was bite down on something that had been saved.

It was after four o'clock when he'd said he had everything he needed. He was offering me a handshake when I asked him if he'd like to come to a service that evening. He'd earned the invite. I told him the Apostles of Jesus' Word were coming down, and the service was going to be a "light unto the world." He half-smiled and took off through the yard with heavy steps. "If you get there before I do, tell them Ellis Clifton invited you," I hollered to him. He stopped for a second but didn't turn around. I smiled and waved just in case he might.

When I got to the temple, the fella was standing outside waiting on me. His hands were in his pockets, and he was digging in the gravel with his shoes. His shirt was crisp, and he'd made time to shave. He had a new tablet with him and a new pencil. When I put my hand on his shoulder, he didn't flinch, and we walked inside, down the middle of the aisle, and up to the front. I got more than a few ugly looks my way as I parked us right on the first row so *he* could see. Miss Esther and Mr. Jim had their tambourines ready, just waiting on the Spirit to arrive. The two men, brothers I think, from the Apostles of Jesus' Word, were already at the altar, stuffing white cloths into the glass bottles on the table in front of them.

The service started with a blessing. Tom Randall was asked to offer up the opening prayer instead of me. I was being put in my place, punished for letting him in close when we agreed not to, but these two days had been a fellowship and wasn't that how it was all supposed to be?

Everybody bowed their heads and stretched their arms out, palms up to the sky. We asked for "open hearts" and a worship that would be "pleasing," and then almost all of us shouted "Amen." I never opened my eyes the whole time to see what the fellow was doing, but I heard that pencil scratching on the tablet.

Miss Esther offered a shout of "Glory to God," then the two men at the front lit the cloths on fire with stick matches. The tambourines trembled and some of the women, maybe it was Mrs. Randall and Eliza, struck out into the aisle, swinging themselves around and singing "Mercy, Lord."

The man to the left of the altar stuck his right hand into that flame palm and all. There it stayed while he closed his eyes and leaned his head backwards. Every once and awhile he'd take his hand out of the fire, hold it above his head, and shout "Thank you, Lord."

The man on the right picked up his bottle and held it to his face, first one side, then the other, touching the glass to each cheek. The flame reached above the crown of his head. Then he set the bottle back on the table, put his right finger and thumb into that blaze and pulled some out on his hand. He put all that glory in his mouth and swallowed it.

The temple couldn't hardly hold all the shouts and songs after that. Miss Esther dropped her tambourine and fell backwards into the pew. The stomps made the glass windowpanes rattle in a fury. The folks that were the visiting Apostles closed their eyes and wept.

The next thing I knew Mr. Wells's hand had ahold of me, gripping my arm in a ball of white knuckles. When I looked at him, his eyes were pinched tight and his jaw, clenched. He'd dropped his tablet and pencil on the floor.

Now I'm not certain why that young man grabbed me like he did. It might be that he was just scared of seeing them men loving and praising in the fire, but I hope it was the Spirit that got ahold of him and wouldn't ever let him loose.

Goodbye Alice

Her shoes are shiny, her dress is not yet wrinkled, and her bangs are still secured by a tortoise-shell clip. She stands in front of the television watching cartoons. Clare stands because she listens to her mother: *prevent wrinkles—no sitting until the car ride.*

She hears her sister walking up the hall in her high heels. Did she see the pink, heart-shaped stickers stuck to the soles? Clare doesn't know for sure, but just because she isn't allowed to wear heels yet doesn't mean she isn't allowed to touch them.

Her sister calls for their mother. Clare listens. It's about accessories. It nearly always is. She can never find *this* purse or *those* earrings or a matching scarf. This time it's the purse. She can't find the small, black leather bag with the strap that looks like gold paper clips hooked together. Of course she couldn't find it. It's hanging on Clare's shoulder. There are things Clare needs to carry, too. Her shell-shaped mirror, strawberry lip gloss, and purple velvet change purse, she has to carry those things. Now was not the time to jam them into her backpack. She needs something dressy and grown up. This purse, swiped from her sister's closet, is perfect. People will see her at Rolling Acres Christian Church, and they need to know she belongs.

She heard her mother and sister talking last night in the kitchen. They assumed Clare was in bed, but she was really hiding in the living room, listening through the wall. At only seven, she'd learned to press one ear to the wall so she'd hear what was happening on the other side. It didn't take her long to discover the most interesting conversations occurred when people thought she was sleeping.

Like the time she heard her father explain how the neighbor's son, Darryl, lit his mother's cat on fire. Clare's mother shouted "Oh, my Lord," followed by a rant of questions about why somebody hadn't done something for Darryl's mental condition. After all, he'd set a section of his parent's backyard on fire last summer. The flames jumped the shared driveway, but Clare's father'd been home, saving the day with the garden hose.

Clare wasn't too upset about the cat. He'd scratched her face once when she'd tried to stuff his face in a bowl of milk. The cats on TV always drank milk.

Her mother said something about Mrs. Shirley's daughter, Alice, and a funeral. Mrs. Shirley, a member of their church, was Clare's Sunday school teacher last year. To her, Clare was "just the best little thing" in class. Never put up a fuss about anything. Walked in and sat at the table with her children's Bible and a smile on her face. Even though she wasn't Clare's teacher anymore, she'd give her peppermints on Sunday mornings. Clare didn't realize Mrs. Shirley was a mother. She was just the nice old lady with the candy.

"Of course your sister's going with us," she heard her mother say. After that, their words came too fast through the wall for Clare to keep up.

Her sister marches into the den, smashing papers and tubes of lipstick into a shiny silver clutch. She throws the bag on the couch, and walks behind Clare to get a magazine from the coffee table.

Lately, she's been too mature to watch cartoons with her little sister. She insists on flipping through the pages of magazines like those women on television—the sophisticated women with cemented hairdos and flawless faces, the ones who'd have an "after dinner drink" with their husbands. She'd been Lizzy for the past sixteen years, but she now refuses to answer to anything other than Elizabeth. Except when Clare calls her Eliza-death. She always responds to her sister then.

The pressure of her stare burns through Clare's wool dress and into her back. Clare's cheeks flush hot. She knows her sister sees the purse on her shoulder, but she keeps her eyes fixed on the bears dancing on the screen. They wear bright pink tutus and ballet slippers.

"If we weren't getting ready to leave, and I didn't think Mom would make me put you back together again, I would smack you to the ground," Elizabeth says, turning one shiny page after the other.

Clare doesn't open her mouth. Their mother appears from the hall, both girls glad to see her for different reasons.

"Let's put on your coats," she says.

Their mother, in a black dress with a simple strand of pearls clinging to her neck, should've been on television. Not one loose hair or a piece of lint anywhere. Women compliment her often, as if they've almost forgotten, or forgiven, where she comes from.

Before she was a wife, Elizabeth's mother and then Clare's mother, she was Sandra Lane, daughter to an adulterer who abandoned his family for his employer's younger sister. The event didn't cause Sandra's mother to lose her mind because it was mostly gone already, but it did make Sandra's life worse. Her mother became more suspicious of women, including her daughter, forbidding her to wear anything other than oversized denim pants and sweaters. No cosmetics or hair treatments, sneakers only, and no dentist appointment to repair a chipped front tooth. It was a wonder, a miracle really, she was saved by Clare's father in high school. Everybody said so. They married three weeks after graduation, after he paid for her to have her tooth fixed. She was a nice enough girl, and fell on hard times for sure, but what he, a handsome young man with a bright future, saw in her, people couldn't put a name to. He must've been an angel put on Earth just for her.

Her mother pulls a small but heavy black wool coat from a hanger in the closet. Clare removes the purse strap from her shoulder and sits the bag by her foot.

"You are not taking it," her mother says, buttoning Clare's coat to the top, choking her into fashion. "It's not appropriate for a little girl to carry a woman's purse."

She looks at her daughter, and Clare, not turning away, squeezes out a tear.

"Well, you can take the purse in the car, but you'd better leave it there when we get out," her mother says. She turns the television off with the remote control, and an attractive woman evaluating her two daughters is reflected in the dark glass.

One tiny tear was all it'd take. Clare knew how to handle her mother to get what she wanted.

Although she has never been to a funeral before, she's seen one on television. She remembered seeing only grown-ups, and they all looked sad. Some of them cried. Her mother must've considered her a grown-up, too.

It's a long ride to Clare, so she feels has enough time to validate her belongings. She unzips the bag and removes her change purse. The purple velvet so beautiful and soft, she rubs her fingers over it then shakes it. She knows the contents: three quarters, four dimes, and two pennies. The quarters came from her mother as payment for cleaning her closet, she found the dimes under the cushion in her father's recliner, and the two pennies were change from her lip gloss purchase. She pulls out the lip gloss, unscrews the top, and brings the tube close to her nose. The scent of strawberry candy and make-up is exciting. She rubs the sticky mixture over her lips, smacking them together, the way she'd seen her mother do when she applied her coral red lipstick. She digs the shell-shaped mirror from the purse. Perfect.

Clare knew when they'd arrived at the church by the way her mother turned into the parking lot. She'd use her left hand to flip the sun visor up and into its place while her right hand rotated the steering wheel. Then she would mash the gas pedal, and their gray Volvo charged up the hill. Clare loved that part of the ride.

The front parking lot is full, so they drive around the back of the church where the cemetery is. Clare sees something that looks like a tent standing between some of the graves. The cemetery is the best place for hide and go seek. On Wednesday nights, if the family made it to church, Clare and her friends were allowed to play back there. Not really allowed, but the grownups didn't say no. The kids ran in between the maze of gravestones, laughing and poking their heads over and around gray blocks until chubby Kevin Clayton tripped in a mole's hole and knocked out one of his front teeth on somebody's stone. He squalled like a baby, his mother went crazy, and Clare's father said no more games in the cemetery.

Clare's father owns Ramsey Volvo and Used Cars. When he travels to view new models or pick up a used car, he brings home gifts for his girls, including his wife. Sometimes he'll call her "his girl," which makes Elizabeth gag and Clare smile. The last time he went on a business trip, he returned with a talking doll. Her name was Misty, and Clare loved her until the batteries went dead, and her mother kept forgetting to buy more when she went grocery shopping. Misty now resides face down under Clare's bed with an empty gumball machine and her sister's old pogo stick.

He's in Chicago, but he'll be home in three days. He calls every night to talk to his wife. He asks to speak to Clare, but she doesn't like to talk on the phone. It makes her sad to hear his voice so far away. Elizabeth refuses to speak to him on the grounds he's keeping the current love of her life from getting through.

Their mother finds a space, parks the car, and turns to her daughters. Examining Elizabeth first, she plucks a few strands of brown hair from her coat. Clare, always in the back seat, requires no further attention at the moment.

"Be very quiet when we go inside. Don't speak unless spoken to," their mother says, her eyes focused on her youngest. Clare's cheeks burn red again, frustrated and embarrassed at her mother's refusal to recognize her transformation today.

As they get out, Clare sees more and more cars pulling in. No sounds of talking or laughter as others join in the walk to the entrance. The air is stinging cold. Some women are draped in thick furs like Clare's mother in her chestnut mink. Men keep their hands tucked into their coat pockets until they reach the door where they grasp the cold brass handle to usher in the ladies. Clare notices there is no Sunday bell. Mr. Yardley always rang the bell at church. One time he even allowed her into the bell tower to see how it worked. She bragged about the experience to her friends at her private school. They weren't impressed.

Clare fails to recognize many of the people surrounding her. Not one person is smiling. She shuffles to her mother's side to wedge herself between her and her sister. Here, she'll be safe. Her mother clasps her hand as they reach the door. Clare hears her sister's high heels clap and clunk as she walks across the brass doorframe and onto the tile. They fumble in the doorway, removing coats and placing them on the wooden hangers. Elizabeth touches her earlobes, reassured her diamond studs are still in place. Clare's mother whisks her hands over her dress first, then Clare's, taking her hand again. As they walk through the foyer, Clare's mother speaks in a low, soft voice to the men and women milling about. Elizabeth offers a few words.

Mrs. Shirley shuffles toward Clare, a white lace handkerchief wrapped around her fingers. Her face, red and puffy, reminds Clare of Elizabeth when her boyfriend broke up with her last week. She'd collapsed on her bed after the tragedy, sobbing and flailing on the bedspread. Clare brought a cool washcloth into her room, and her sister rolled over, jerked it from her hand, yelling, "Leave me alone."

Kneeling in front of Clare, Mrs. Shirley kisses her cheek. "She's the prettiest little thing," she says. "Both of your girls. Pretty." Her husband, gripping her hand, pulls her up, and they back away. Clare, wanting to speak, raises her eyes toward her mother, but she shakes her head no, pulling Clare through the foyer with Elizabeth following. Their mother stops at a tall pedestal, writing all three names in perfect script. After taking a folded piece of paper from the surface, they walk inside the sanctuary.

They creep along with the rest, a silent line of lowered heads. Clare's mother holds her hand as they shuffle to the altar. Clare stares at the lady's back in front of her. Her dress is navy blue with tan stripes. Her legs, round and thick, are wrapped in dark pantyhose, her large feet crammed in dark blue shoes. A long, curly string dangles from the bottom of her dress. Clare reaches to tear it off, as she'd seen her mother do many times, but her mother squeezes her hand.

A long, shiny gray casket lies before them with a young woman's body tucked inside. She wears a lavender dress with a high lace collar and ruffles on her sleeves. Clare wonders if the lace is choking her.

"See the high neckline?" Elizabeth leans forward and whispers into Clare's ear. "It's to cover up the rope marks. Mom heard Alice hanged herself from the ceiling fan in her dorm room."

Elizabeth disappears behind their mother and returns her stare to the toes of her shoes while Clare's eyes focus on Alice. Their mother sniffles, but Clare doesn't look up. Her little chest brushes the casket's edge as she leans closer.

The young woman's face, a glowing white, has red circles painted on her cheeks and purple eye shadow on her lids. Clare's gaze moves down the body, stopping at the young woman's hands. Her right hand, resting on top of her left, is milky white with dark purple lines crossing underneath the skin. Her fingernails, painted a pale pink, make Clare wish for the color herself. She wants to reach inside the casket and feel, touch a dead hand.

She strains her neck to the side, attempting a look farther into the casket to see the girl's legs, but they're hidden in the dark. Clare's mother squeezes her hand, using more pressure this time, moving them away from Alice.

They join the line of others, extending handshakes and somber hugs to the family standing by Alice. Men and women on both sides of the line are crying. Some weep loud and gasp for air, hiccupping with open mouths.

Mrs. Shirley, shoulders hunched and trembling, nods her head. Clare offers her small hand like the others, but Mrs. Shirley fails to take hold. She leaves her arm extended until Elizabeth pushes her forward. "Just go on," she says, her fingernail digging into Clare's back.

At the end of the line, their mother ushers her daughters to a back pew. Before sitting, she smiles, mouth closed, the flawed tooth haunting her, and whispers, "Chicago" to a man and his wife nearby.

No Mr. Betram, their regular pastor, no lady to play the organ, no choir in blue robes with red sashes. Clare's church is unrecognizable. Her mother reads the paper from the pedestal like it's one of her romance novels, only inches from her nose while she mouths the words. Clare stares at her sister as she digs in her purse, wishing she could do the same. The taste of strawberry lip gloss long gone by now. Clare takes a Bible and Prayer Request card from the back of the pew in front her. She taps her sister's arm, pointing to a pencil near her, which she hands over after an impressive eye roll.

She needs answers to some important questions. She'd see Mr. Bertram tomorrow morning, so now is a good time to make her list.

1. What do people wear in Heaven?
2. Will I have my own room?
3. Is there television?

Her mother takes the Bible from Clare's lap as she finishes writing her last and most important question. Clare folds the card into a small square and presents it to her mother, who places it inside her purse.

A man's voice booms from the podium. He's the young pastor from the university chapel.

As he speaks, women sniffle, and a man toward the front has a coughing fit. Clare's mother nods as the pastor offers enthusiastic words of consolation and explanation. Elizabeth picks at her dry cuticles while Clare thumps her shoe on the tile, her toes tingling and burning from lack of movement. Her mother, horrified, looks at her with wild eyes and pinches the back of her arm. Clare scoots her back against the pew, crossing her legs at the ankles like a good girl, and rests her hands in her lap.

After claiming a final "Amen," the young pastor invites everyone to follow him outside. He strides down the center aisle, his black robe unzipped and flowing, exposing his tie, navy blue with a scarlet cross in its center with rays of fairer scarlet bursting forth. Like a vision in a dream, out of focus, but the colors radiant and swirling, he secures the gaze of all attendees.

Clare climbs onto the pew cushion, hoping for a clearer view, but her mother catches her, ordering her down with the stare of her pale blue eyes. As the casket passes by their row, the three of them exit the pew and join the procession of others shuffling their way outside. The mourners stand, circling the dark green tent, the chairs underneath filled with those who knew Alice best or loved her most or both.

Mrs. Shirley faces the casket. Clare wonders how long this part is going to take.

Outside is still cold, the temperature having dropped a few degrees since the service began. Nobody'd thought to retrieve a coat from the foyer, or maybe they decided it was unacceptable to leave the crowd. Clare shivers, clinging to her mother's hand. Her mother'd taken hold of it as they walked. Soothed, Clare grinned and interlaced her fingers with her mother's. She'd been forgiven for her earlier offenses.

The young pastor raises his hands into the air, palms up. He invites those gathered to bow their heads. He prays, open-eyed, for "everlasting peace" for Alice and her loved ones. To Clare, his voice seems angry, and he uses too many big words, making her thankful for Mr. Bertram's gentle way.

Then it is over. Everyone's duty fulfilled, they begin to walk away. Back to their cars to begin their own lives again, moving past this brief disruption.

Clare notices more chatter as people move toward their cars, some forming small groups. She hears lunch plans and sees toothy grins. Some of the women brag about what dish they'd taken to the Shirleys.

She hears another someone ask her mother why her "good-looking husband" hadn't been with them. She explains he's out of town on a business trip.

Clare wishes he'd been with them, especially when they were in the cemetery. He'd have wrapped the edge of his suit coat around her to keep her warm. He'd do things like that for her sometimes.

Their mother unlocks the car, and they climb inside. Elizabeth, who'd been instructed to retrieve the coats, throws them in the back seat, burying Clare underneath the pile. Clare digs her way out and reaches for her purse. She opens the shell-shaped mirror to evaluate her face. Her droopy eyes mean she needs a nap, but otherwise she'd held together well.

Elizabeth and her mother talk all the way home. They discuss the service, the people, the clothes, and the weather. Clare, fading in and out of consciousness, is not invited into their conversation. Instead, she sits with her head relaxed to the side, catching a few glimpses of the outside:

An old lady still in her housecoat walking from her mailbox with nothing in her hands.

Mrs. Shirley was rude to me today when she didn't shake my hand like she did everyone else.

A buzzard picks at a dead animal's guts on the side of the road.

Can worms and bugs dig through the casket and get to Alice?

Mr. Lawson's cows standing in the field.

Daddy never did take me to visit the farm like he promised.

When Clare hears the sound of the garage door rising, she's reenergized. She runs into the house, tosses her sister's purse on the kitchen counter, missing the fruit bowl by an inch. She'll retrieve her belongings later when she's looking for something to do.

In her room, she pulls off her dress and tights, piling them on the floor. Her mother walks in her room. "Hang up your dress, fold your tights, and put them in your drawer," she says.

Clare huffs as her mother walks out of the room, but she does as instructed because she listens to her mother.

As she stretches the neck of her dress around the hanger, she can't stop thinking about Alice. She wonders if her mother would make her wear that kind of dress when she dies, an itchy-looking one with a high collar. She'd have to ask her sometime.

The phone rings. Clare's mother brings her the cordless. It's her father, wanting to talk to her like always, and today, she returns his favor.

"Hey, Daddy. How many more days until you come home?" she asks, walking in a circle around the blue edge of her rainbow-colored rug.

"Shortcake," he says, "be there before you know it. What can I bring you? You know, something little, so as not to spoil you too much." He joked about spoiling his girls, especially Clare since she was the baby.

"I saw the prettiest pink nail polish today, Daddy. Can you bring me some?" she says.

"How about I take you with me to get some when I get home? To make sure we get the right one?" he says.

"Okay. I'll tell you all about it. Love you." She gives the phone to her mother, leaning against the doorframe. She takes over the conversation as she walks up the hall.

Clare stands in front of her dresser, making faces in the mirror. A toothy grin, a frown, a mad face. All the faces her mother claims are ugly and asks her, "What would you do if your face froze that way?"

Climbing onto her bed, she lies on her stomach and tucks her arms underneath her pillow. She releases a tight yawn, closing her eyes. The voices of her mother and sister carry down the hall and into her room. Their words surround her, covering her like a bandage. Today she's been a child and a young woman and it's been exhausting, so she sleeps. The best kind, deep, peaceful, and pure. Second only to a permanent sleep, like Alice's.

Sweet Smoke

They hadn't spoken this morning or shared anything more than a few words since he was sent home months ago. Iva clenched her teeth at her husband Raymond as he rolled himself out of his recliner and shuffled by her to reach the percolator on the stovetop. Two, three, four teaspoonfuls of rationed sugar swirled in his coffee. With his good hand, he took the last two drugstore doughnuts from the box, leaving it on the counter. He returned to his refuge in the living room, sprawled himself back into his chair, slurping and grinding while he leaned toward the radio. For now, the network signal was clear, and the reports from the warfront were due soon.

Iva sat at the kitchen table pulling a calming breath from another cigarette and arranging her stationary: the crisp white paper with the gold foil at the edge, the cream-colored envelopes, her supply of sharpened pencils. Another letter to Sister Sylvia, the missionary serving in China.

Raymond, a fifteen-year veteran of a paper mill, had been sent to basic training, got hurt, and the U.S. Army released him of his duties. He was in training to be a mechanic, the jack buckled, and his hand was crushed under the truck. He wasn't away six months. Through the screen, Iva'd watched her husband wave his good hand to the man who'd given him a ride home. Before he was through the door, she'd slapped her open palm on the back of his head, pulling his face forward, his mouth close to her own. He jerked backward, blinking wildly as if to clear his vision. Stumbling in the empty space between them, Iva caught herself on the doorframe and faced her husband.

"Need to sit a minute. Get myself together," he'd said with his back toward her as he dropped his luggage by the sofa and sunk his trim body into the chair cushion in the living room.

"Fine." Iva'd walked into the kitchen and smoked a cigarette over the sink, admiring the rich scarlet of her freshly painted fingernails. "It'll come back to him," she'd whispered to herself then. "Like his mama said—she'd seen the devil in us."

Iva wasn't the devil. Neither was Raymond. But they both had demons for a while. Creatures of lust deep inside, twisting their bodies and minds, forcing them into battle against one another. It'd always been that way, even when they were courting and everything was supposed to be peach blossoms and sugar sweet dreams.

The first time either one of them caught a glimpse of what they had was when she met his mother. After supper, the old woman took them into her garden, pointing to this flower and that plant. All the while, Iva and Raymond squeezed and pulled at one another's hands. When his old mother walked past the corner of the house, Raymond yanked at her arm, spinning her around toward him and slamming his mouth into hers. She pressed him right back, their front teeth hit, and she chipped off the bottom of his front tooth. When he pulled away, he smiled, and she threw her head backwards, laughing.

All he did now was read and listen to the radio. He would drive an hour away just to get his good hand on a city newspaper with the war news in it. He read them all as soon as they were available and saved them. The living room was scattered with papers, some stained and mangled, piled into corners and on tables, and stuffed into his chair by the radio. He gained weight, too. His belly swelled but never surged like it used to before when he breathed deep into his anger and passion. He poured sugar into his coffee by the spoonful and devoured sweets while he combed through each paper. He ate and ate but never got full.

Iva glared at her husband's profile as he stared at the radio. The glob of fat dangling from his chin, the bulge around his middle, large enough for him to rest his hands upon while he listened. His thoughts, it appeared, consumed with frustration and envy for all the young men he met and those he hadn't yet that got to stay and learn and go off to the Pacific or to Europe to fight, left him tired. There was no energy left for her. His lust for her had died and absorbed into his shriveled hand, leaving him with nothing to say and no motivation to act.

She returned her thoughts to the day's task, the letter. She slid a cigarette from the package, lit it, and left it resting in the ashtray while she rummaged through her stationary case. She found the instructions from Superintendent Doyle, the leader of her church's conference. Last year, her Sunday school class was selected to write to the missionaries the local churches supported. She'd been assigned to Sister Sylvia in China. She read through the guidelines again.

Offer a blessing. Share church news and happenings. Scripture verses are acceptable. Personal information should be limited. End correspondence on a pleasant note.

She refolded the paper, tucking it in the back of the case. She was proud of her first letters, how she'd adhered to the rules. It didn't bother her not to get a reply then. Like attending church, she did as she was expected, hoping it'd count to somebody, for something.

Once, Raymond asked her why she even bothered going to church. "You can't be saved," he'd said. "You don't believe in all that hocus pocus any more than I do."

It was true. She didn't believe in God. Even as a child hearing the stories of Moses and Noah, she didn't believe. She couldn't touch them and their lives didn't touch hers. She'd grown up attending services. It was just something they all did, so she kept on with it. She told Raymond it couldn't hurt to go, but she never told him that she got to be somebody else there. Like Betty Grable in a picture show, she could make people believe she was different than what she really was. The ladies accepted her as one of their own—a wife, a Christian, not yet a mother, but that would come they insisted.

Children would have ruined them, and, in turn, been ruined themselves. Children needed something they didn't have and couldn't get. Once, on a summer evening as the thick black air seeped through open windows, Raymond claimed he wanted a son. His confession came after his second glass of bourbon. He yelled at Iva for being too thin, which kept him from having his son. She'd said nothing, continuing to search her vanity table for an envelope she misplaced. The fact that she appeared not to be listening or caring infuriated him. She knew it was the bourbon talking. Whenever the bourbon talked, she went and poured herself a glass. She smiled when he called her a lush, and he smiled at her when she took an even heavier swallow. His chipped tooth had never been corrected, and it captivated her when she saw it, reminding her of the cost of their passion.

That summer evening she dismissed him by patting him on the shoulder as she walked out of the bedroom, and he lunged after her in the hallway. They fell on the floor, together, angry but not, and pushed each other away, yet all the time becoming closer. Nothing happened there, not at that moment. They slept for a while, or rather, Raymond slept. She lay on the carpet, with her arm stretched across his heaving belly, counting the tiny black cracks in the white plaster ceiling until she drifted into sleep, too.

They awoke after midnight. Starving, they went to the kitchen. No time for place settings or coffee, they ate pork and beans out of the can, scraping the metal sides with their spoons as they dug. The half a ham from lunch was ripped apart between their fingers and thumbs, and they passed the milk jug between them, swallowing and wiping their mouths with the backs of their hands afterward. She belched, he laughed, and they climbed into bed.

Iva now heard the click of the radio knob. The newsman had given Raymond all he knew: "U.S. advances in the Pacific"—not much and veiled in static. Time for another newspaper.

She watched him fight, squirming to fit into the now too small jacket he didn't need since the air was thickening, warming into a new season. It was the pocket he wanted, a hiding place for his disability. He didn't bother to wash his face or brush his teeth. No hat. He wore a pair of old work trousers that he took to some old woman to let out since Iva refused.

His eyes never cut toward her. She watched to be sure. He slipped his bare feet, hinged on swollen ankles, into a pair of scuffed loafers, the pair he wore before he stopped doing any yard work. With a gentle pull, he closed the door behind him, making sure to keep the screen from slamming also. Iva stabbed her pencil onto her clean sheet of paper, fracturing the tip. The quiet sounds, the weakness in his hands and his spirit, angered her. She stood, inhaled a clean breath, and ran the fingers of her right hand through her curled and set hair. Discarding the loose strands on the carpet, she took her seat, determined to start and finish the letter without interruption.

My Dear Sister Sylvia,

I hope my letters have found you well. Though I have not received any replies from you, Superintendent Doyle thanks us for our support to you all and assures all of us ladies that our messages are getting through. I wish I might hear from you so you could tell me what you see. Remember in my last letter how I asked you where you slept? Surely you thought that was a silly question, but we were told you sleep on the floor with a mat. I hope you find it restful. I have found the floor to be comfortable and have had some of my best dreams there even when I was a child.

Again, I ask your forgiveness before sharing my next thoughts, and I hope you do not think me inappropriate. Maybe you do, and do not write to me because of it.

A few weeks ago, the doctor removed the bandage from Raymond's hand. I'd been waiting to see what it looked like—I believe I told you. I was disappointed when I made him show me because it looked better than I expected. His index finger is missing, and his whole hand has shrunk. The yellow on the black skin means it's healing, so it's going to be all right. His doctor told him he'd never be able to use it like before, just favor the left hand now. He could learn to use it to run the wood chipper at work, but he hasn't. All he does is eat and sit by the radio, and I hate him for it.

I wish you'd known us before, before all of this. Maybe you wouldn't have liked us then either, but we couldn't help what we did to each other. Not love, something else was between us. Anyway, whatever it was is gone for good I think. Maybe some of it is my fault.

I am thankful that I have enough sugar—it is rationed here now, did you know? I used to make three buttercreams a month to give away at church, but now he uses too much in his coffee, all day long to stay awake. Anyway, I can make two cakes, and the ladies still love them, praising me for the gift. When they ask me how Raymond is, I say "As sweet as sugar." This makes them smile and feel comforted. They don't want to hear the truth, no dirty or depressing stories about a soldier. When I am with them, I am an actress in a picture show.

You must think I am a vulgar woman. You need not tell me so.

Please be well. Write me when you can. I tell you these things not to upset you but because I have no one else to tell.

Truly yours,

Iva B.

Iva stared at her writing, surprised how she'd written darker, heavier, almost cutting through her fine paper. Her thin fingers reached for the burning cigarette and brought the filter to her mouth for a few weak puffs. Her words conjured the memories, lifted them up and out of the page, and when she exhaled, they and the white smoke clung to her.

After she'd met Raymond's mother, they stood at the altar in two months. They'd sworn to love and honor. She'd said "obey" to him through squinted eyes and gritted teeth, but she did say it, which he never let her forget. Over the years, she never let him forget he was supposed to be the provider, so there were always folded bills in her change purse for cigarettes, sugar, and writing paper.

Camel Regulars were her choice. She'd been offered her first when she was fifteen and never stopped. It was her uncle, the one who had just lived with a woman for a while who gave it to her. To this day, she is still infatuated with the package. The camel in the golden desert, stopped, but heading somewhere; places she might never see. If she just kept smoking, she was part of the scene, so that's what she did.

She lit the first one while the coffee was percolating, and she lit the last one after she got into bed. Only once did she catch something on fire: Raymond's cheek. It was just a little burn, hardly a blister came up, but his rage ripped their little bedroom apart. He called her vile names, flipped her nightstand, shattering her porcelain lamp against the wall. It had been a wedding gift sent all the way from Texas from an aunt she never met, but everybody said she resembled. Her anger slept until then. When she saw those white pieces on the floor, she grabbed the biggest piece she could find, one with a good, ragged edge, and flew at Raymond, waving it in her hand. He backed away but was stopped by the dresser. She held the porcelain to his throat, and he gripped her wrist, her fingers numbing from a lack of blood flow. They stared at one another, neither willing to give in, not yet. Seconds passed into a minute as their chests heaved and jaws tightened. He exhaled, forcefully through the nose, and it was over. The fury had exhausted their minds but not their bodies, and they gave into one another, submitting to the passion they shared that existed in the middle of contempt and devotion.

The next morning, she found herself naked and intertwined with Raymond on the floor. The first thing she did was slide herself away from him and walk to her side of the bed. There were her Camels, still in the pack, waiting for her on the floor. She lit one, breathing in deep and heavy. She left the cigarette dangling from her lips while she looked around the room.

"Not too bad this time," she said, running her fingertips over the fresh cut to her knee.

It was she who'd always loved sugar, and it was Raymond who hated it. He'd taken his coffee without any, not even in his iced tea in the summer. He'd never eaten sweets, not the slightest pinch of her buttercream cakes did he taste. They'd fought about that too, the cakes she baked, sometimes three a week that went uneaten. She'd give one to a lady at the church or take one to a shut-in, a feeble old man or woman hoping for company to arrive while waiting to die. There were many times her confections went into the garbage pail out back for the raccoons to ravage. She couldn't explain it. Maybe she wasn't sure herself. All she knew was the way she felt when she held the metal scoop and leveled the flour into it. The crack of the eggs made a sound she could never duplicate, and she let her mind drift as she stirred the batter. First, counterclockwise with her right hand then clockwise with her left. Her sight blurred as she lost herself in the creamed mix flowing perfectly into the round pans, shined by a thin layer of grease. The heated air from the oven washed her face when she pulled down the door to set the pans inside. For that moment, she was warm and red-cheeked and at peace.

While the cake baked, she could write her letter to her missionary and get back to her Camels. She didn't smoke a single cigarette when she baked, which she more than made up for once the oven door closed. Really, she wrote for her own soul, not Sister Sylvia's, and not in a way she could explain if she had been asked. She wrote the letters she would have liked to read if she ever got any. She wanted her to think she was interesting, not just any old housewife or mother. Sister Sylvia had read plenty from those people, but Iva was certain she was the only Camel-smoking cake baker who loved the church but never believed.

Iva folded the letter into precise thirds, and packed it in the envelope. She made sure to print the address, no cursive on the envelope. Those were the rules. As she wrote, her thoughts turned to Raymond's mother. His sister called last month to say their mother was sick, but Raymond refused to visit. He said his sister lived too far out in the country, too far away from the world, and, besides, he couldn't bear to go without listening to the radio for two days. So it was Iva who'd called his sister to say they weren't coming, and it was Iva who wrote the get-well note to his mother. His mother had never cared for her, she knew. For years, she'd said Iva and her son weren't good *to* each other, weren't good *for* each other. But Iva wrote the note. She did the right thing.

Iva heard Raymond's car tires roll over the gravel. He'd gone to Nye's Drugstore, in town. He mustn't have had the energy to go any further. He stumbled coming in the door, couldn't be bothered with lifting his feet anymore. There was the rattle of the newspaper crushed under his arm, the sound of his keychain sliding across the top of the doughnut box.

He set the box on the table in front of Iva and pulled a pack of cigarettes from his pocket, not Camels, some brand she'd never heard of. She didn't look up. There was nothing to see.

Opening the lid to the doughnut box, he hooked two frosted circles onto his thick middle finger and shuffled into the living room. Iva heard the groan of Raymond's recliner as it adjusted to his body. Click. The radio was on. The advertisement for Bromo Seltzer—the repetition of the name set to the rhythm of a locomotive barreling down the tracks.

Iva used her stationary case to push the open doughnut box onto the floor. With the knuckles of her index fingers, she dug into the corners of her eyes. When she looked at the back of her hands, she approved of the black mascara stains in the creases.

She walked over to Raymond, who sat embraced by his chair, and snatched the newspaper out of his hand. He said nothing, only one eyebrow lifted slightly, and he raised the volume on the radio. Still clutching the paper, she went into the kitchen. She returned with the paper, transformed into a torch. She started in the corner, lighting the stacks as quickly as she could. Raymond had risen from his seat and was trying to conquer the flames with one hand and a sofa cushion. She'd made it back to his chair and was ready to light it when she had to drop the last corner of the torch before it burned her.

Iva stood in the center of the room while Raymond wobbled around her, panting and slapping at the flames with the cushion. Singed flakes of newspaper floated through the air like snow.

With the last of the small fires extinguished, Raymond collapsed in his chair. The heavy stench of scorched paper and fabric sealed the room. Iva thought the smell cleansing and breathed in heavy, expanding both lungs.

What she'd expected to happen did not. He didn't call her names or grab her or lunge at her as if ready to attack. His eyes didn't meet hers, and they didn't contest one another. There was no craving, no desire for her or their life anymore. When he returned to his seat and leaned his ear close to the radio, it was confirmed.

Still standing in the center of room, her hand clinging to a fragment of newspaper, all that was left of her torch, Iva's mind flashed to a new scene. She watched herself pull her suitcase from the closet, pile a few clothes into it along with her measuring spoons, and what was left of her porcelain lamp.

It never did work after that night she'd burned his cheek and they'd fought, but she couldn't bring herself to throw it away. She'd glued what pieces she could together, and it stood. If she turned it just the right way and didn't look too close, it seemed as if it'd never been broken.

Closing her eyes, Iva imagined taking a couple of newspapers from Raymond's stack to wrap it in. Long for them more than me, she thought. She took her suitcase into the living room and sat it down next to one of the burned circles in the carpet. She put on her hat, coat, and gloves, lifted the suitcase by the handle, and then threw it across the room. At this image, Iva tossed the scrap of paper remaining in her hand into the air.

Opening her eyes now, she saw Raymond, his mouth open, staring at her. His chipped tooth, once a playful reminder, was yellowed by his indulgence in sugar and coffee. The luscious black hair she used to pull in passion and in rage was thinning, exposing streaks of pale pink scalp.

She couldn't do it. She wouldn't do it. She hated Raymond for making her consider leaving, for stopping the fights, and for ending their hunger for one another. Maybe it'd satisfy him for her to leave, but she wasn't in his way. All these months, he simply moved around her, acting as if she weren't really there.

Iva exhaled, waking herself from the thoughts and the images of Raymond. She shook the newspaper scrap from her foot, the one she'd flung into the air as if it had been her suitcase. As she walked back to the kitchen, her naked feet crushed the debris underneath, coating themselves in silver ashes.

She selected the single doughnut that remained secured in the box and took a bite. The sweet crunch of the frosting soothed her for moment, but it left a thick film on her tongue and in her throat.

She tossed the remains in the box and returned to her seat.

She'd send two letters to Sister Sylvia today.

Desire

Sue's pigeon-blue Tercel rattled to its stop, the right side's tires over the line into someone else's space. She was still having trouble parking. Her father was supposed to help her practice and fix the noise coming from somewhere under the hood. A clacking sound, sort of, when she mashed the gas pedal or pressed on the brake. She was counting on him to take a look soon.

She cracked the door, the seatbelt taking its cue to let her free. She watched it move slowly along its track until it reached the end on the doorframe. The water rushed over her feet when she stepped out. The rain had come up over the ditches, keeping the parking lot from draining at all. She'd not thought to wear boots. They wouldn't have gone with her outfit anyway. She climbed back in, across her seat to the passenger's side to grab her purse, bumping her head on the way out. She covered her head with the purse and ran to the door. She was more excited than nervous, scared some, but not too much. After all, she'd wanted to visit this jail since she was a little girl. She'd never told anybody. It wasn't something to tell.

The door cast her reflection and she looked, hard. She smoothed a crease in her denim skirt and teased her lemon-yellow bangs with her fingertips. She pulled a piece of skin from the corner of her thumb with her teeth.

She stood straight, though she wasn't sure why, maybe to look older, like she'd done all of this before. So maybe they'd think she knew the drill. She didn't know, not at all. How she thought things should be she learned from television or the movies. Old black and whites she and her father watched together when she was younger when her mother worked nights. They'd sit on the couch, usually somewhere in the middle to avoid the holes Sue's mother had burned with her cigarettes on the armrests. Now that she was thinking about it, it'd been a while since she and her father had watched one of those movies together. Once he started seeing Theresa, the latest girlfriend, and Sue got her driver's permit, they spent even less time together. But they might've gotten together soon for a burger or something. They could've made the time somewhere in between their separate lives.

Her skirt pocket held the letter still in the envelope with James Madison Corrections stamped as the return address. She'd brought it along as proof.

Sue Rose,

Sunday is visiting day. Bring me some chewing gum and a pack of Viceroys. Joey said he'd bring you if you wanted or if the car wasn't running right. Come around 11 in the morning.

—Your Dad

Had she remembered the gum, yes, it was in her pocket. She patted it to be sure. When she went to the store to get the cigarettes, Mr. Barnes smiled at her. "It's a shame about your dad," he said. "A real shame. Been there over a month now, right?" Sue nodded, and Mr. Barnes charged her for the cigarettes but not for the gum.

People did stuff for her now. Kelly Trent's mother brought her a chicken casserole last week, the same kind she brought the day after Sue's mother had died. The night it happened, Sue could hear her father yelling into the phone. Sue's mother called home before she left work, they'd fought, and she wrecked. Flipped the car six times somebody'd said.

Even Uncle Randy came from out of town to mow the yard. They all meant well, she knew. They were just trying to help, but all those things just reminded her how different it all was. Her life and her daddy's. It wasn't all that great before, but it was better, somehow, than what was happening.

She'd be fine coming alone. No need to bother Joey. Besides, she didn't want to hear his voice again, to talk about how it all went down. He was her father's friend, not hers. They worked at the garage together. He'd been the one to call her and let her know. Her father had called him first, which she still didn't understand. She'd been home. She could've gone somewhere and done something, but it was Joey he'd wanted to talk to right then. She'd hated how he called her "sugar" over and over, telling her how her daddy was fine, just caught up in a little trouble with Theresa. He wouldn't be home for a while he'd told her because the police were going to keep him until it was time for court.

"I'm Sue Morris," she said as she stepped up to the desk. The two officers behind the desk looked at her, grinning.

"Who you here to see, doll?" the younger officer asked. He removed a white handkerchief from his pocket and rubbed it along his forehead and over his lips. "I believe the rain's made it worse out, hadn't it?"

"Yes, sir," Sue said. "Nelson Morris. I'm his daughter." She stared at the picture of the American flag behind the desk. For some reason she couldn't look at either of them. Her voice sounded funny. She knew it. Her lips weren't working like they should. It was like she couldn't control them. Maybe it was the way the officers were looking at her. Now she wished she'd asked Joey to come with her.

"Sign the form," the older officer said. He stood and walked to the front of the desk beside Sue. "I'll need to look in your bag." He reached for the strap on Sue's shoulder, but she was able to grab it and put her purse on the desk before he could touch her.

"Anything in your pockets?" the younger officer asked. He stood now, too, watching as his buddy poured her belongings on the desk and tapped each item with his middle finger. When he found her compact, he cradled it in his left hand and opened it. He held the mirror a little above his head and moved a few strands of hair around to help cover a balding patch in the center of his scalp.

Sue took in a deep breath and dug into her skirt pocket with her thumb and index finger. She pulled out the pack of gum and handed it to the officer. He reached for the gum, making sure to brush her hand with his own.

"Well, this is my favorite kind. Your daddy won't mind if I get me a piece first now will he?" he said. Sue shook her head no and smiled, a little, she thought. Her lips tingled a bit and still didn't feel exactly right.

The older officer instructed Sue to pack her things back in her bag, and he put his arm around her. "I'll take you down to the meeting room," he told her. The younger officer returned to his seat, smacking his gum.

To Sue, the meeting room looked like her high school's cafeteria. There were orange tables and chairs and one drink machine in the corner. The officer left her there and told her he'd be back in a minute and she should just find herself a seat.

There were plenty of empty chairs for it to be visiting day. Sue chose a table for four in the corner next to the drink machine where she took her seat. She liked the buzzing sound it gave off. She hung her purse on the back of one of the empty chairs, crossed her legs under the table, and waited.

There were two others in the room. An old woman, still in her housecoat it looked like, sitting across from a man. He was younger than the woman, Sue believed, but not by much. The man held a rag and rubbed it over his eyes every few minutes. His lips struggled to form the words she couldn't hear.

A large round clock hung over the entrance to the room. She watched as ten minutes ticked by, then fifteen. Her heart beat through the center of her chest like the second hand on the clock. They beat together, sometimes. She could feel it. She lowered her eyes to see the polyester fold between her breasts move forward then backward. She wondered why she had never noticed this before.

The door in the corner of the room opened, and the older officer, the one who slid his arm from her shoulder to her waist walking down the hall, stood behind her father and led him into the room.

He walked to her carefully, one determined step after the other, and took the seat opposite her own. She'd thought, for a second, about standing and moving toward him for a hug, but it would've been awkward and not something either of them had done before, that she could remember.

"My lucky number," he said, not looking at Sue but to his shirt pocket where his inmate number ending in three was stitched in black. The fingers on his right hand tapped the table to some tune she'd never heard.

"I brought your cigarettes," Sue told him. She dug into her purse, taking longer than was necessary for her to find them. She handed them over with a book of matches, and her father grabbed them and tucked them into his shirt pocket.

"Save these for later," he said. "I'll take a piece of gum, though." Sue handed him the pack. He picked at the wrapper, slow and deliberate, and pulled out one piece. He tore it in half and tucked one half with the cigarettes and slid the other out of the foil and threw it in his mouth.

Sue watched him chew, his jawline protruding with each grind. Good looking even though he was old, her friends told her. Mostly it was Kelly, who'd say she wished her father looked like him and what a shame it was he couldn't find a decent woman to take care of him since what happened with Sue's mom.

"The preacher came by the house," Sue said. She looked to the left of her father at the clock on the wall. It never was easy for their eyes to meet, one embarrassed of being a father and the other embarrassed of being his daughter.

"What'd he want?" her father asked, with his voice raised and eyebrows lowered.

"Just to see how I was. He told me to come by the church and let him know if there was anything he could do." She'd hesitated before telling him, but she couldn't think of anything else to say. The silence between them was torture.

"Nosy," her father said. "Plain nosy. Don't you tell him a thing." He adjusted his position in his chair, arching his back.

Fine, she thought. No problem there. She didn't know anything anyway. Only what Joey told her. His words throbbed in her mind. "Bad checks," "Theresa's fine," "Jail," and "No bail."

"I'm working on getting all this cleared up," her father said. "Be out before you know it. You need anything, you call Randy." He started to stand.

Sue looked toward the corner of the room. The old woman was still there, visiting with her inmate, who'd been able to tuck his rag into his shirt pocket by this time. Sue thought she'd seen him smile once or twice.

Sue stood, taking the strap of her purse and hanging it over her shoulder. They'd missed their chance, she thought. Her mind, swirling and angry. This should've been their time to get everything out. Who'd know about it besides them? Start with Mama's wreck. Tell the truth for once—he'd made her crazy, accusing her of cheating on him because he was out of work then and didn't have anything better to do, and she lost control of the car. It wasn't because she hadn't been paying attention like the trooper said. It wasn't her fault.

And if he'd been writing bad checks, just say so. Or, was it Theresa's idea? She was fine according to Joey. Of course, she was too smart to get caught. Sue never liked Theresa anyway. Her teeth were yellow, and she was too old to be wearing cutoffs.

"Bye, Daddy," Sue said, his name awkward passing through her lips. He winked at her, maybe. He'd done it a few times before. She watched the older officer remove his paws from the newspaper he'd been sharing with his fellow guard at another table and walk toward her father.

Her father turned from her, leaving her to see only the tightness in his shoulders as he went.

A dull ache seized the back of her throat, yet she watched her father's exit. The older officer unlocked the door, motioning for her father to step inside. The officer followed, and he pulled the door closed behind him.

Sue made it down the hall, this time free of the old man's grip. In front of the desk where the younger officer sat, she did not walk fast or slow, but at her regular pace. When he told her to have a good day and called her honey, she didn't look down or blush, but kept her eyes straight ahead.

It was still raining, but she decided not to cover her head with her purse. She walked to her car with purpose, appreciating the squish of the water inside her shoes with each step.

Inside the car, she took a napkin from the glove box and dried her hands, then took what was left and wiped the mascara from underneath her eyes without looking in a mirror.

She cranked the car, turned the radio off for the first time, and took off through the parking lot. On the main road, she rolled her window down, about halfway, and looked at her spotted reflection in the side mirror. She was determined not to stop until some street, somewhere called out to her, wanting her there no matter what the reason.

She puckered her lips. I am a pretty girl, she thought.

Play

Susan and Donna pedaled hard. Susan's purple gumballs, tucked in a rag, rested in her metal basket, and Donna's peanut butter cups and polished Mary Janes were tucked in hers. They could slurp water from someone's spigot on an outside wall if they needed to. The spring air was sweet but heavy, wrapping them in damp gauze. Each day newer than the next; the rusty-colored paths bearing the burden of their bicycles.

"Isn't it more fun in our bare feet?" Susan asked. She was one month older, but smaller. Her dark brown hair, thin in sections, spilled everywhere.

"It hurts," Donna said. The corners of her glasses were tinged with orange dust. A barrette—her mother's idea for bicycle rides—caught her yellow bangs.

"No it doesn't," Susan said, her knuckles pink and relaxed.

Side by side they rode. With Susan's red bike frame and Donna's green, they looked like Christmas. They looked ahead and around, waving to each other when necessary. Susan stood on her pedals coasting down the hill; Donna tightened her grip on the handlebars in the gravel. Susan tried catching a squirrel speeding ahead of her; she caught a blister. They got to the tree—the big one with other people's initials scarred into it—and they stopped.

Susan dumped her bike on the grass, spilling the purple gumballs into the green. She found one and ate it but left the rest. She followed the curves of the new letters embedded in the tree trunk with her index finger just like she did with the names on the gravestones behind the church. The "W" followed her favorite, the "S." She never found her parents' initials there, together with a plus sign or a heart. She searched the tree each time. Donna's mother told the story of how the first letter of her name was engraved by Donna's father, which gave Susan the idea.

Donna sat on the ground, wiping the moistened dust from her glasses with her mother's white handkerchief.

"I know what we should do," Susan said. "Let's go to the cemetery and play hide and seek." Her voice coarse but soothing like sand. Gumball juice escaped through the corner of her mouth.

"We always do that," said Donna. "I've got some money. Let's go get ice cream sundaes and eat them inside where it's cool." She secured the glasses over her ears, folded the handkerchief and returned it to her skirt pocket.

"That's because you're a scaredy cat," Susan said, standing over Donna. "You always have fun after we start playing." She spit out the gumball because it'd lost its flavor, and retrieved a fresh one from the grass. She blew on it and popped it in her mouth.

"Fine," Donna said, brushing her backside as she stood. "It's your way or no way."

Susan jumped on her seat before Donna; her bicycle, resting on the tree trunk. Susan waited as Donna climbed on. Her peanut butter cups lay softening in their wrappers.

Today's after-school route was different but like always it ended at the cemetery where they played across the road from the home of Mrs. Carrie Brimwater. People thought they knew a little about Mrs. Carrie Brimwater, and they were certain her mailbox was ugly. The red metal flag, faded and deformed, drooped on the side. The box itself used to be a shiny eggshell when the Martins lived there. Now it was copper-colored with streaks of white, infected.

No one saw her enter or leave through her screen door. No one bumped into her in line at the bank, and no one asked her how she was after church because she never came. If people looked for her, she might be visiting her husband.

"Do you have the note?" Susan asked, not bothering to turn her head to see if Donna knew which note. She spit her gum, and it flew backwards, grazing strands of hair before sticking itself to the dirt. Her freckles grew darker in the afternoon sun. She whistled, for a moment, stopped. Susan and Donna had conquered the craft, but girls shouldn't whistle, so they didn't, at least in front of Donna's mother who'd told them so.

"I hid it in my desk," Donna said. Her cheeks an uncontrollable pink.

At school they sat next to each other, sharing a pencil case they bought together at Rye's Pharmacy. Susan wrote bad notes and Donna read them. Susan survived on fried chicken for lunch. It was barely secured in brown paper before her mother tossed it into a rusted pail, but Susan enjoyed it, snapping the bones to suck the marrow. Donna devoured two peanut butter rectangles, a red apple, and a cookie she split with Susan.

At the corner of the road, Susan and Donna stopped again, allowing the school bus to pass. Susan grunted at the children's heads hanging out the windows. Those children suffered, their afternoon playtime limited and their energy extracted by the swirling haze consuming the bus's insides. Susan and Donna never caught the bus because they lived too close to the school, a privilege and a curse.

"Come on. Pedal," Susan said, not demanding herself but Donna whose blue eyes focused on the back of the bus. Donna lifted her tender feet from the road and positioned them on each side, gazing at her shined and inviting Mary Janes.

The cemetery was at the edge of the town. This one was not the one at the church but another where sometimes guests came to visit and sometimes they didn't. It was a big square with rows of stones large and small. Some were cracked and scraped, some were shiny and smooth, some were topped with hardened lambs, waiting, guarding.

The entrance gate was open, always. They rode through and abandoned their bicycles.

"I'll count, and you hide," Donna said. Facing the way they entered, she cupped her hands over her glasses. "One Mississippi, Two Mississippi, Three Mississippi." Her numbers were precise and pleasant until the end, "Fifty."

Susan exploded forward. She ran way, way back to the other side of the lot. The uneven and cumbersome ground was no match for her accuracy, leaping over lumps and darting to the side of stones in her path.

She arrived at the set of stones she thought best; the ones family couldn't wrap their arms around when they tried. She looked left, right, and back again trying to recall each game and where she hid before. Choosing a medium square, she sat, pulling her knees to her chest. She stroked the start of her blister with her fingers, beginning to pick and pry for it to come up.

She heard Donna coming. Her numbers were clear and the drier blades of grass cracked under her. Susan twisted her body and leaned to watch her.

Donna was close, at times, but moved away quickly when there was no immediate result. She walked too far, down to the gardener's shed. There was an open spot in the snowball bush, a good place; she used it last spring. She crept toward it, peering over its top, nothing.

The gardener didn't mind them playing. He watched them often, sitting on the concrete stoop of the shed smoking a cigarette. They were not allowed to sit on the tops, he told them, but traipsing on the tops of covered bellies was fine.

There was the cluster of small stones, all side by side. Susan discovered the possibility of lying flat behind them. Donna told her later, "Good one." Donna tiptoed there, but found no sign of Susan's orange shirt in the gaps of the stones.

Donna let out a frustrated blow through her nose. She began to weave between the stones, not leaving one untouched.

Susan watched her become four stones away then three then two.

"Gotcha," Donna said, sitting.

"Oh, well, it took you longer this time," Susan said. "Your turn." She stood, not wiping stuck grass from her behind.

"Wait. Look," Donna said, pointing. "It's Mrs. Brimwater. My mother calls her *not right*."

"Why?" Susan said, half whispering while sitting on the flat top of someone's resting place, her thin legs dangling in wrinkled slacks. She bounced her feet, alternating, on the last name. Her toes blinked.

"I don't know. I heard her talking to someone on the telephone," Donna said. She slipped her hand into her pocket and withdrew her saved treat. She tore the wrapper, lifting one peanut butter cup, her finger on the top edge only and her thumb on its bottom. She bit it, the milk chocolate barrier released the creamed peanut butter onto her tongue. In seven bites, she finished one cup, protected the other in the wrapper and saved it in her pocket. Her heavier thighs extended the skirt, and the outline of the package pressed forward.

"Let's get closer," Susan said. Making themselves as small as they could, they crept behind the large stones and moved toward Mrs. Brimwater, never removing their gaze from her.

"Follow me," Susan said.

They positioned themselves behind the stone to the left of Mrs. Carrie Brimwater's husband. They were completely hidden except for a small portion of their faces peaking from the side, like a two-scoop ice cream cone.

Mrs. Carrie Brimwater stood straight as some sticks in front of her husband. Her white dress, tight in the shoulders, hung loose at her ankles. Her yellowed gloves made her fingers look fat. Coral lipstick shined on her mouth, making her powdered face pale and cracked. Her hat, too small for her head, sat perched, ready to fly away. Formerly large, round eyes stared at the lettering on the stone. She swallowed often and hard.

Donna looked up at Susan, gesturing with her eyes for them to leave. Susan rolled her eyes but nodded and stepped back. She planted her hands on Donna's back and pushed. Donna, falling forward was exposed. Trying to stop herself, she knocked her glasses from her nose.

Mrs. Carrie Brimwater's eyes were now wide but terrified. She stumbled back, over her feet and a hollow spot in the ground. The girls watched her yellow hands cut through the air searching for anything to catch her. Her feet and chest were forced backward while her neck, stiff and strained, pulled forward.

The edge of a stone met her middle back. Her body slumped to the side, brushing the sharp edge of the stone's foundation. She looked like a spool of thread come unraveled.

On her knees, hair knocked loose, Donna patted the grass for her glasses. She found them unharmed and fit them to her face. Her toe, stubbed—the pink tender skin ripped and raw as her foot struck the bottom of the husband's grave. She stood, turning to face Susan, whose brown hair was pulled tight at the scalp and now secured behind her ears.

Donna pressed her tongue to her mouth's roof, then out a crack of her lips, the weight of peanut butter inside.

Susan stepped close to Donna, brushing her hand against Donna's skirt. As if attached to one another in a three-legged race, they slid their bare feet through the grass.

Mrs. Carrie Brimwater rested face up. Her lips were parted, and she was panting. She was missing a shoe. It lay on its side near the hollow spot. Her dress, the bottom now gathered between her knees. Her silver hair, unpinned, spilled everywhere, yet her gloves were secure. The too-small hat fit nicely on top of a concrete vase where it was caught.

"Hello, hello," Mrs. Carrie Brimwater called, patting the ground with both hands hoping to find a foot nearby. "Girls, help me. Get somebody to help me."

Susan and Donna crouched by the woman's feet. She was straining her neck and squinting her eyes trying to make out their faces.

Susan looked at Donna, her mouth hanging open and her eyes tearing up with the surprise of what she'd done. She moistened her lips with her tongue. "What should we do?" she asked. "I don't want a whipping for this."

Donna inhaled a calming breath through her nose and then took hold of Susan's hand. Together, they took a step backward from Mrs. Carrie Brimwater, who was still panting for someone to help her.

Donna offered Susan her handkerchief. "Wipe your eyes," she said, her voice demanding. Susan did as she was told, giving the white cloth a swipe by her nose, too.

"Somebody else'll find her," Donna said, stuffing the dirty handkerchief back in her skirt pocket. "Let's go." She turned toward the cemetery entrance.

Susan stared at her friend for a moment, admiring her stride between the gravestones. Susan ran to catch up with her, and the two girls fled on their bicycles.

There Isn't Any More

Hazel helped Bill, her husband, into his suit coat, leveling the shoulders with heavy hands. With her face turned from him, she slid his silver cigarette case into the breast pocket. Her eyes, the color of fresh mud he'd once told her, were weak. She feared they'd tear up or glaze over—they'd expose her.

"Now don't you spend all day fiddling around with those snowball bushes," Bill said. "I need you to have the basement ready for the O'Dells to come by and look at. They're coming by first thing tomorrow morning. Remember, I have to visit the bank to sign the rest of the papers for the house, then Myers Insurance Agency, and then back to the office."

Hazel nodded and offered her right cheek to Bill for a kiss, which he failed to notice because he had occupied himself with verifying the location of his cigarette case, wallet, and car key. The screen squealed as it opened to release Bill and then again as it returned to its place. Hazel shut the oak door and made her way to the kitchen to clean up the breakfast dishes.

It was day three in the new house. After five years of living in White's boarding house, Bill had saved enough money to put a down payment on a two-story home. He had a nice office job at the furniture company that had opened several years ago, and Hazel had contributed a little money to their cause by selling her needlepoint pillows at church bazaars. She was quite talented at stitching birds; in fact, she blushed when the ladies told her they could hear sad coos released from her mourning doves.

Bill had decided to take in boarders since the new house had a full basement. With the added income, he could pay off the mortgage earlier. Hazel liked the idea of giving a young couple the option of living somewhere besides Mrs. White's boarding house, which really was just a single-story box filled to the brim with whining cats. Earlier that morning while preparing the coffee, Hazel believed she'd seen the fat calico jump from the potato bin onto the kitchen counter, yet when she turned around, the cat was not there.

The basement was large enough for a kitchenette and a bathroom, and Bill had a plumber coming next week to help set everything up. In the meantime, he'd instructed Hazel to tidy things downstairs as best as she could. There was a wrought-iron bed already in place. All Hazel needed to do was wipe the dust off of it and put on a set of sheets and a quilt. She was supposed to move their night table downstairs, too, since Bill was getting a new one for them at a good price through his company. She was to wash the basement's windows, both inside and outside, as well. The window washing had been her idea. She wanted the O'Dells to notice how the sunlight would brighten up the whole basement. Somehow, it made the concrete walls look pretty.

Hazel placed her dishtowel over the sink and walked into the living room. It was almost time for her favorite soap opera, "Our Gal Sunday." If she turned the volume all the way to the right, she would just be able to hear it while she worked in the basement.

Yes, folks I said Anacin. That is spelled A-N-A-C-I-N. You will be delighted with the results.

The radio had been a wedding gift from her brothers and sisters. All eight of them had chipped in, some more than others she was certain, to buy the newlyweds the radio. When it was delivered to the boarding house, Mrs. White allowed the men to set it in her kitchen. The noise would be a bother, she said, but she would just suffer it so the couple wouldn't find themselves even more cramped in their bedroom. After about a month, Hazel told Bill the only time she got to choose a radio program was when Mrs. White took her bath on Tuesdays and Thursdays. Bill didn't seem to care. He'd said the radio was a nuisance and an impractical gift for a young couple with no home of their own and no money to speak of.

Practicality all the way. That was Bill Morris. Nothing was ever bought on time payments, except for the new house, the realization of which was wearing him thin, home from the office for dinner at noon, and supper, always with cornbread on the side, at six-thirty. Some said he was peculiar. Really it was only Hazel's sister, Beaty, who called him peculiar, but Hazel was certain there were at least a few others that thought that way about him. Hazel could see how people might think so, but he really wasn't peculiar, just a no-nonsense man. Everything he did at every moment had to have a reason behind it, some purpose to be done, or it wasn't worth his while. There'd been a peak of this practicality in the last few months, and especially the last few days. He'd taken on a mortgage and much of the renovations for the basement apartment, combined with his regular work at the office, so there never seemed to be just the right time for Hazel to tell Bill the news—she was expecting.

Hazel was clearing the photograph frames from her night table when the doorbell rang. She evaluated herself in the mirror. Dressed only in a striped housecoat with a slip underneath, but her hair was washed and pinned and her face was clean. Her brown eyes, bright and wide. She was presentable, enough, for whomever was at the door, probably a salesman pledging to make her life easier with the touch of one button.

The doorbell chimed through the house, again. Hazel walked faster.

"Coming, coming," she called. As she made a detour into the living room to turn off the radio, she heard the announcer:

Can this girl from the little mining town in the West find happiness as the wife of a wealthy and titled Englishman?

Somehow, she always does, Hazel thought before rotating the dial.

"I could hear the radio on the porch," Iris said as she stepped into the house. Iris was married to James, Hazel's brother. She was a petite woman with fine clothes, but her presence was sour and her voice curt.

"I like having it on, and I like it loud. It drowns out everything else," Hazel said, ushering Iris into the living room.

"No doubt you were listening to those absurd soap operas with their fickle men and moaning women."

"Never mind them," Hazel said, offering Iris a chocolate from the candy dish. "What brings you by?"

"James. It was his idea I drop in to see how you were feeling," Iris said, declining the treat with a wave of her hand. "You were looking worse for wear the other day, but you seem all well now. Not a trace of a cold." Iris lowered her thin eyebrows, glaring at Hazel.

Hazel had asked Iris to drive her to Dr. Price's office the day before yesterday. Bill had told her she looked a bit peaked, and she'd better get to the doctor's before she got worse. They had too much to get done this week. Besides, he couldn't afford to get sick and have to stay home from work.

Iris pulled into the driveway promptly at 9:30 AM. Hazel's appointment wasn't scheduled for another hour, and it only took about twenty minutes to drive into town, but Iris was a cautious driver to say the least. Every now and again Hazel would accompany Iris to purchase weekly groceries, and while Hazel was certainly thankful for the ride, she did wish Iris would drive a bit faster. When Hazel dared ask her about her driving style once, Iris replied, "Well, at least I know how to drive," and then she added her customary statement, "When you rush, you risk."

When they arrived at Dr. Price's office, Iris said she would be quite comfortable waiting in the car while Hazel received her diagnosis. She didn't want to catch anything that was catching. She'd driven the entire time with her scarf draped over her mouth and nose. Despite Iris's driving, Hazel was still quite early, but she decided to sit in the waiting room. She flipped through a last year's magazine, stopping briefly at each page containing a cartoon. When she heard the nurse walking up the hallway toward her, Hazel closed the unfinished *Life* and returned it to the coffee table.

No, it wasn't a cold or the beginning of a bout with pneumonia. Hazel, at thirty-five, was expecting her first child. Dr. Price had just lit his second cigarette when he delivered the news. He determined she was a couple of months along. She was an otherwise healthy gal, and she should have Bill lower the clothesline for her before the next load was hung. Hazel tried to listen to his instructions, but her mind was elsewhere. How had she missed it? Well, her cycles were often irregular; that was true. With five years of marriage and no children to speak of, she'd thought having children to be impossible. Now, with the move and the new house and preparing for live-ins, well, she just failed to notice. Bill wouldn't be satisfied this was the best time, especially since they'd gone so long without children.

While neither of them could actually recall wishing for a child, both Bill and Hazel assumed one would come along eventually. It wasn't until about their third year of marriage that Hazel thought anything about being a mother at all. She figured something was wrong on her part. Bill never mentioned children. He'd play with his nieces and nephews if enlisted, but he never pursued their company. He was far too busy with his work and trying to make a good impression with the executives at the furniture company. The process of wanting or acquiring children was an issue best left unaddressed anyway. Hazel recalled the time when Iris told her mother she was expecting. While waiting for one of their grocery trips, Hazel sat in the living room and overheard Iris on the telephone in the hallway talking to her mother. Due to her mother's poor hearing, Iris shouted into the receiver, and her mother shouted in return. She heard her mother shout, "Don't you tell a soul." Hazel remembered the darkened expression that shadowed Iris's face as she walked into the living room.

It would've been natural for Hazel to begin thinking about her own mother at this moment, but she didn't. Her mother had nine children and no husband to speak of, not the traditional kind. He provided only sadness and aggravation for his wife and children. He dropped in and out of all of their lives as it suited him. Sometimes he'd stay for two days, other times a week or so. It seemed like as soon as he left another child came along. They came one after the other. Her mother even had a set of twins, a pair of boiling pink boys, Hazel bottle-fed while her mother healed. To this day, Hazel couldn't be certain what happened to her father. Only flashes of a dark, lanky image existed in her memory. It was her mother who'd raised them, and they helped raise each other. As a young girl, Hazel hated her mother's weakness and how she allowed her children to suffer because of it.

The heat of the examination room, the swirls of Dr. Price's cigarette smoke, and her concerns about Bill's reaction absorbed her concentration. She needed to get home and finish unpacking and setting up the house for any potential boarders. Bill had placed an advertisement the newspaper, which meant the house needed to be ready in a moment's notice.

As Hazel walked out of the office, she decided there was no need to tell Iris; she'd be disturbed by the news in one way or another, or she'd offer nothing but advice for the entire ride home. It'd be better just to let her think she had a cold. Besides, Hazel needed the time to herself to plan how she was going to present Bill with the news.

Now Hazel had known about her condition for almost two full days. With Iris across from her, Hazel's face flushed a convicted red. "I really do need to get back to the housework," she said, standing, her eyes concentrated on the front door.

"Fine. Like I told you, it was James's idea for me to come," Iris said, brushing a piece of lint from her lap. "He'll be relieved to see you've recovered so quickly."

"I'll tell Bill you said hello," Hazel said, half-waving to Iris in her car. As she watched Iris's gradual turn onto the main road, she thought of Bill. When he'd gotten home from work on the day she visited the doctor, he was in a terrible mood. Something had happened to a number of important invoices at the office, and then when he stopped by the bank to sign the rest of the paperwork on the house, the bank officer had already left for the day. He stomped through the living room and turned off the radio, yelling, "You could get a lot more done if you didn't pay so much attention to that nonsense." He'd been so worked up he even forgot to ask her about her appointment with Dr. Price. He wasn't himself, and she just couldn't bring herself to tell him. She'd planned to tell him last night, after supper. She'd prepared some of his favorites, cubed steak with gravy, green peas, and cornbread, of course. He never tasted much of it, though, saying he had brought home some work from the office, and he wanted to work on the cabinets for the kitchen in the basement while there was still daylight left.

Tonight for sure, she thought. He'd been in an almost pleasant mood at breakfast, she'd have the basement looking nice and tidy for the O'Dells to see, and she'd tell him with a grand smile on her face. She refused to allow her own anxiety to show. She'd explain now was a good time for them to have a child because of the extra income from the boarders. Their child would also have his choice of second-hand clothing from all his cousins.

On her way back to the bedroom, Hazel switched on the radio in time to catch Sunday's husband, Lord Henry, tell her:

You, my dear, are a caged lioness.

Indeed she is, Hazel thought. We all have that in common.

In the bedroom, she retrieved a new package of white bed linens from the closet. She placed it on top of the cleared night table, lifted the table on each side, and headed for the basement. Stopping to listen for a moment, she heard only a commercial, so she made her way down the steps.

The sheets hadn't been pinned properly, and they unfolded into a large bulging bundle in her arms. As she began to fold them, she felt a stinging pain in her stomach; a loose pin or two must've caught her skin through her dress. She found the two pillowcases and began stuffing them when she felt hot liquid trickle down her inner thigh. She lifted her dress, discovering blood. She saw no sign of stains on the sheets, so she left them as they lay on the bed. With one hand, she held the bottom of her house-coat between her legs as she climbed each step with determination. She must be careful to avoid making a mess.

Hazel shuffled down the hallway into the bathroom and climbed into the empty tub. After half an hour, there were no more stomach pains, no more blood, no more anything. She took a rough washcloth to every inch of skin, scouring between her fingers. She washed her hair again, digging her fingernails into her scalp. Out of the tub, she perfumed and powdered and extracted too many eyebrow hairs. She opened her eyes wide, gazing in the mirror as she applied a thick layer of mascara to her dry eyelashes. She pulled on a tattered bathrobe, one she kept hanging on the back of the bathroom door, and gathered her clothes, compressing the garments into a mound barely visible in her hands. With the afternoon passing and her emotions and womb dried up, she needed to do the wash and get back to work in the basement. There was supper to prepare before Bill got home.

Hazel hung her clothes out on the line although it was more difficult to open the pins this time. No need to ask Bill to lower it now, she thought. When she threw her slip over, it didn't catch and fell onto the ground. It didn't matter anyway. She figured on throwing it out. Though she had scrubbed it over the sink with soap and cold water until her fingers burned, the stain only spread. It didn't disappear. She had hoped she could save it, though. Bill's mother had given it to her as a wedding present. It had yellowed only slightly; otherwise, it was smooth and shiny. That slip was the final garment Bill had removed on their wedding night.

She remembered how warm and ready she was when he placed his finger under the strap and slid it off of her shoulder. It had ended up on the floor that night, but now it was on the ground, stained, ruined, and waiting to be thrown away. She dropped it in the burn barrel with the coffee grounds and yesterday's newspaper.

When Hazel heard the shrill bursts from Bill's car horn that evening, she knew he was playing with her. She joined him by the door, her heavy chest bumping into him.

Bill stepped to the side. "Everything has been taken care of," he said. "We're all set for the house." He handed her a pack of chewing gum. "Heard the jingle for it on your radio the other day," he said. "I'm trying to *woo* my girl like it says." Hazel returned his foolish grin with a half-smile and shoved the small package into her apron pocket and returned to the kitchen.

Now he was in a good mood. He whistled while he hung his coat on the rack and stumbled while removing his loafers. Hazel listened as he walked down the hall and stopped at the basement door. His sock feet thumped on the steps.

"This looks nice," he yelled from the basement. Hazel continued peeling carrots over the sink, wiping leftover skin caught in the grater on her apron. She heard the basement door close, and Bill entered the kitchen. He moved close to her side and this time she backed away.

"I think the O'Dells will like the room," he said, snatching a peeled carrot. "They'll like it even better when the kitchen and bathroom are set up, but they'll just have to use their imaginations for a while. They're still young enough to do that." He split the carrot with his front teeth. "I'm going to work down there this evening after supper," he said, grinding what was left. He then took a slice of cornbread from the tin by the counter. "What are we having tonight?" he asked between bites. "Hey, this cornbread from last night is even better today. Do we have any more?" He turned to evaluate the contents of the tin, hoping there may be another piece, but he found it empty. Hazel placed the grater in the sink, wiped her hands on her apron, and walked out of the kitchen. She sat down in the chair by the radio, which she'd turned off some time ago. She slid her feet from her slippers and stared at her toes.

"That's all there is. There isn't any more," she called to him.

Stay

She stole money from her granny. Just a twenty-dollar bill here and there to make her stay worth the while. She'd earned it, really. The fifty bucks her granny handed her every other Friday wasn't close to paying for all she did to help out the old lady. She half expected to get paid in two Moon Pies and a grape Nehi like Travis, the pimple-faced boy who mowed the yard.

All the morning she'd listened to her granny rant over how late she'd talked on the phone the night before. They were on the porch. It was Friday. Fridays were for pulling weeds and sweeping. All the bedclothes had to be done on Friday as well, if her granny was up to helping with the folding.

"Lord have mercy, Erin. I know you heard me telling you to hang up the phone last night," she said, pointing with her arthritic finger to a bright green leaf between the rails on the porch. "Hard enough to rest as it was— thinking about that poor Culbert family down the road. House was broke into last week. Good thing they weren't home." She lifted her cane, aiming the rubber bottom at the false flowers growing nearby. "Get that one there and there's a few dandelions over by the step."

Erin despised the cane. If her granny used it like she was supposed to, everything was fine, but when she used it to point, the back of Erin's neck flushed hot. One more thing for her to fetch or wipe or fix.

She sat in her old rocker with the chipped paint on the armrests pitching herself back and forth with the fat heel of her good foot. Her hair looked the same, grey and white pieces frizzed up and in loose curls all over her head, but she'd make Erin take her to the beauty parlor tomorrow anyway to have it reset. Little blue flowers dotted this housecoat. It was the one she wore when she was expecting company. People did seem to stop by on Fridays.

Erin took the metal trash can lid from the carport and flipped it over to catch the weeds. When it'd fill up, she'd walk it down the hill and pitch the weeds in the woods. Through the brush she could see the white trailer at the bottom. Nobody she knew lived in it, but every now and then she'd hear laughing.

Her granny had three toes cut off because of problems with her "sugar." Erin hated when people called diabetes "sugar." It sounded ignorant. Her daddy told her she'd need to stay with her grandmother a couple of weeks to do for her because she wouldn't be able to do for herself. At the time, she thought being with her mama's mama might help take some of the sting off—her mother being treated in a psychiatric hospital. A couple weeks turned into the whole summer. It was close to the middle of August, and she'd have to take the bus back home next week to get ready for junior year.

It was after ten by the time Erin dumped the last load of weeds over the bank. "Get ahold of the root or not at all" was still repeating in her mind. Her granny gave her instructions on how to do every little thing.

"Open and close the cupboard doors by the knobs. No need to slam them shut. Well, you don't have to tear them off."

"I'm on a well out here. You don't need to flush every time you make water."

"Pick out what you want from the refrigerator before you open it. Can't afford to run up the electric."

"Little girl, in my day we didn't go around showing our navels."

"Don't walk in the middle of the living room carpet. I like fresh vacuum tracks for company."

"Do you love okra? Your mama loves okra. You better believe it."

More than anything else, mostly, Erin hated when her granny used the word *love* like she did. No, she didn't love okra, but she did like it though she never took one tiny nibble when her granny tried to give her a piece. She heard the grease popping in the skillet the day she arrived. Some old man her granny knew picked her up at the bus station and dropped her off to a house, and a woman she hadn't seen in two summers. She walked right into it, too. Her granny, out of the hospital for two days, stood by the stove with one fat foot shoved in a powder-blue slipper and the other wrapped in white strips of gauze with a scarlet shadow near the toe. Erin had stood at the edge of the kitchen, dividing her glances between the flipping and stirring on the stovetop and the scarlet color climbing its way through the dressing resting on the linoleum. Before unpacking what she later learned were "trashy" clothes, she'd read a pamphlet on amputation, elevated the woman's burden, and applied a fresh bandage, all without gagging. When Erin reminded her she was supposed to be on bed rest for at least a week, her granny shook her head and ordered Erin to recheck the bandage. She didn't want it unraveling when she was "right in the middle of something important." Erin redressed the foot four extra times in her first week, but it took a visit to the doctor's office, the voice of a man, for her granny to understand she needed to stay off of her foot. "He's good to me," her granny claimed on their way home, tapping her hand on her leg.

Erin returned the trash can lid to the carport, and grabbed the broom from the corner. She dragged it around the side of the house to the porch, which needed a good brushing every morning she was told. Sweeping was tolerable as long as there were no surprise inspections. She'd spend a good half an hour tearing apart webs and tossing the leftovers, their homeowners included, into the yard. How much dust and red dirt gathered overnight on the white planks. Almost as if someone came along while they were sleeping and sprinkled it there. Did her mother consider that type of thing when she was younger and forced to do the sweeping? Erin tried not to think about it. She tried not to think about what her mother might have thought, and she tried to ignore the ache in her gut. She'd eaten little since she moved in, grabbing a cookie or a can of pork and beans here and there for lunch. Suppers were best, normally a casserole or a box of fried chicken somebody dropped off because her granny was "a likeable type," she, herself, often admitted. After the first morning, she'd not eaten another breakfast.

Her granny ate the same breakfast every morning. A bowl of cottage cheese and half a red grapefruit. The cottage cheese was revolting, especially the way she ate it. Erin sat across from her at the tiny oak table somebody's grandfather's uncle carved as one whole piece. Her granny took out her teeth and sat them on a reused white paper napkin next to her coffee cup. She'd clink her spoon on the inside of the bowl each time she dug for a serving of white lumps. She'd stick the whole spoon in her mouth and scrape it clean with her thin upper lip, smacking the glop between her gums.

If Erin finished with the porch in time, she'd be able to sneak inside while her granny was taking her afternoon nap. When her granny slept, Erin could swipe money from her purse or crush up a laxative or two to mix into her food. If revenge weren't required for the day, she'd doze on the couch in the living room. Somewhere between dreams of leather cowboy boots and carnival rides and ghost calls of her name coming from her granny's bedroom, she'd rest.

Late that afternoon, Erin and her granny, both exhausted by their work, slept heavy until well past dark. Erin woke to the request of "a little something to eat and drink." Before going into the kitchen, Erin straightened the throw pillows, each returned to its regular position. She yawned, wide and deep, covering her mouth with the back of her hand. In the kitchen, she pulled the lap tray from the pantry and began to fill the order. There were some leftover chicken and dumplings she heated in the toaster oven. She filled another bowl with a heap of snap beans mixed with a little ham, and spooned the last of the cherry cobbler into a coffee cup. She placed all of the dishes on the tray, wrapped a fork and spoon in a white napkin, poured "a Diet" into a glass filled with ice, and then took everything to her.

Erin was still sleepy, but she dared not fall asleep before retrieving her granny's tray. All of the dishes needed to be rinsed right away, she learned. They couldn't wait until morning, so she did as she'd been told. As she ran the scalding water over the bowls, she heard her granny turn on her television set. Her bedroom was small enough and her bad foot was healing well enough now for her to move around a little.

Erin spread a towel over the dishes, locked the front door, and turned out the lights. At the door to her room, she thought she heard "Goodnight, Erin," but she wasn't sure, so she didn't respond. She figured this might not be a good night to call one of her girlfriends, having kept her granny up the night before. Besides, she was still tired. The more sleep she got, the more tired she was.

She didn't bother washing her face or brushing her teeth. She changed into her nightshirt, slid under the covers, and turned off her lamp. Saturdays started early, and they were busy. She'd have to be ready by eight so they'd have plenty of time to get to the beauty parlor. She'd drive the big brown Taurus to have her granny's hair washed and set and then to the grocery. Saturdays were hardest because everywhere they went Erin met at least five other old women who were exactly like her granny as far as she could tell.

The cry of the screen door being pulled open woke her up. At first she thought it might be another shy neighbor dropping off a note or a card, but it was way too early in the morning. It was nighttime, still. She was sure of it. Peeling back her blanket, she slipped out of the bed, off to the side nearest the window. She tilted her head to see the edge of the porch and two dark figures at the front door.

Her heart beat loud and deep, causing the inside of her ears to begin ringing. These men, these strangers, were going to come inside the house. They were going to stomp on the vacuum tracks in the hallway as they walked by her mother's senior portrait. She'd be able to watch them without their knowing. She'd be the one protected.

Erin flew to her door, locking it just as she heard the front door open. She'd never thought to lock her bedroom door until now. With her ear pressed to the door, she listened and, at the same time, she didn't. She could see a thin line of light reach under her door then disappear. She could hear the crush of the carpet under their boots in the hallway, then the vibration of the crash. They'd stumbled into the small table lining the hallway, the one Erin damaged twice with the vacuum cleaner, once by accident and once not. The table, displayed with trinkets, picture frames, and a glass vase filled with marbles was overturned.

Erin returned to her window, raised the lower sash, and used her elbow to punch through the screen. Her long legs stepped over the blooming azalea bush into the yard.

She looked back for a moment expecting, maybe hoping, to hear her granny call for her, but only the echo of her pounding heartbeat filled her ears. No lights were on at the trailer below the hill, so she made her way through the wet grass to the road where her bare feet met the gravel. She ran fast and hard away from her granny in the direction of the Culbert home, her feet already beginning to numb themselves against the pain.

Work Gloves

In the spring of 1948, Thomas and his Japanese bride journeyed from Yokohama to his hometown in Pennsylvania. Here, they were to begin their new life. It'd been decided they would live with his mother until he could save enough money to buy a house. He'd work at the local grocer's while his wife stayed with his mother in order to learn how to tend an American home. He'd promised his wife the arrangement would only be for a short while, and his mother'd teach her many useful things like how to make the homemade egg noodles he loved so much.

When they arrived at the home, Thomas's mother met them at the front door. Her brown apron covered nearly all of the navy-blue dress she wore underneath. Her arms, plastered with age spots, grasped for the son she had not seen for five years. His Japanese bride remained unnoticed on the step. Finally, the son pulled away from his mother, straightened his tie, and cleared his throat.

"Mother, this is my wife, Fumiko," he said.

"Thomas, she will address me as Mother Reed," said his mother.

She turned her back to the couple and went inside. Thomas gave Fumiko a quick wink and went to retrieve the suitcases from the cab. Fumiko did not go inside alone. She stood on the step waiting for her husband, noticed the chipped grey paint on the shutters, the brown and white dog pulling at his chain by the shed, a thick, too-sweet smell released from white blossoms in the bushes. She wondered why she had come to this place at all.

Six months ago, Thomas convinced Fumiko to leave her father and brothers in Yokohama. He told her he could not make money in Japan anymore. He'd been a fireman at the American base, but now it was closing. Fumiko made a little money by sewing for the officers and their wives, but it wasn't enough to support her and a husband. Thomas insisted they go to the United States. They could live with his mother while he worked. In no time at all they would have a house of their own and a shiny new car. He could make so much more money in his hometown because he had connections there. Although Fumiko knew she would probably never see her father or brothers again, she did not resist. She was his wife, and he was only doing what he thought best for them both. He told her it would be a difficult transition, but she spoke English, and that would help. He told her Americans hated the Japanese. However, Thomas assured her his family and friends wouldn't be like all of the rest.

Thomas shut the trunk of the car and gave the driver a few dollars. With the last bag in hand, Thomas stopped and ushered Fumiko in front of him. She bent down to remove her shoes, but the look on Thomas's face told her she did not have to. As they entered through the kitchen, the smell of burnt wood and cabbage confronted them. The small but efficient kitchen was equipped with a wood stove, and a large pot of chopped cabbage simmered on its black surface.

"Thomas, I've got a loaf of that bread you like baking," said Mother Reed.

Thomas smiled at his mother, then at Fumiko, as he patted his stomach with his hand.

Fumiko wanted to learn how to cook Thomas's favorite dishes. It was not as if she had not tried in Japan, but many of the ingredients she needed were too expensive. There was never enough flour or sugar, but there was always plenty fresh fish.

Fumiko quickly assessed the contents of the kitchen. One stove, one deep sink with a red water pump handle attached, four canisters lined side by side along the back edge of the counter, one small icebox, and one dark oval table with two chairs tucked underneath.

At that moment, it did not occur to Fumiko to worry over the table for two. She did not know she would never sit across the table from her mother-in-law. She did not know that during every lunchtime, for the next year and a half, Mother Reed would force her to stand by the sink to eat her meal if she were offered one. Only during breakfast and dinner, when Thomas was not at work, did Mother Reed allow Fumiko to sit. Even then, she was not allowed to pull her chair to the table. She had to hold her plate in her lap as she sat by the sink.

"*She* will never sit at my table."

This was the only statement Mother Reed ever made concerning the arrangement, and she was serious. She set that boundary on the evening of their arrival as she placed two plates on the table and one by the sink. Thomas rose from the chair to protest, but Fumiko shook her head in resistance. It was important to Fumiko for them to show respect to Mother Reed. After all, they were living in her home. She was older and she must know a great many things, so it did not matter to Fumiko where she must sit. This was to be her home, and she must accept its rules.

"Thomas, take the girl to your room," said Mother Reed, stirring the cabbage in the pot. "I don't want any of her belongings strewn around this house. It's bad enough she's here, but we need not advertise to company."

Thomas said nothing. He picked up the last bag that he'd carried in and walked into the adjoining room. Fumiko followed. As she stepped softly behind him she surveyed the living room of her new home: a wooden stool with a dark green cushion for its seat opposite a brown couch with a black patch sewn onto the arm, and, in the corner, a tall piece of furniture. It had five shelves, and each shelf contained a picture, a book, or a dish. Fumiko wished she could take a closer look. She wanted to see the dishes. She was interested in designs and patterns. In fact, that was all she asked for when she married. She told Thomas that the size and shape of their house did not matter as long as she had beautiful dishes to serve their meals on. Thomas promised he would buy her a set of dishes right after he purchased a house.

Fumiko also wanted to see the pictures and ask Thomas who the people were. They were her family now, and she wanted to recognize them, but Thomas continued to walk at his steady pace, her legs working to keep up with his lengthy stride.

Fumiko followed Thomas into a small bedroom. He said this was to be their room. The bed was covered by a rumpled, yet seemingly clean bedspread made entirely of feathers. Fumiko noticed one of the feathers floating at the side of the bed when Thomas thrust his body onto it. Their suitcases were taking up nearly the whole floor of the room. Fumiko stepped over and between them to get a closer look at the oak dresser against the wall. It had four drawers. As she pulled one out, she realized they were not deep at all. She did not know how she would fit her entire life into two of those drawers, but she knew she must.

She would make a considerable effort to hide her things away in this room. She did not want to upset Mother Reed. She was the outsider, invited in, and she must obey the rules of the house. At that moment, Fumiko believed that if she listened closely to Mother Reed and followed her instructions, she would never have any difficulties.

"Thomas, time to eat," called Mother Reed. Thomas sprang from the bed, gave Fumiko a pat on her bottom and headed to the kitchen. She knew he would no doubt be hungry. She was a little hungry herself. It had been a long time since they had shared a cold ham sandwich on the train.

The three of them ate cabbage and bread in silence. Thomas and his mother were seated at the table, and Fumiko sat by the sink. She kept her head down and stared into her bowl. She listened to her husband and mother-in-law discuss cousins and farming and deaths and births. She heard Mother Reed tell Thomas that some of the neighbors were glad he'd returned home but were not too happy about what he had brought with him. Fumiko directed her eyes toward the table when Mother Reed made this comment while Mother Reed kept her eyes focused on Thomas.

When they had finished eating, Fumiko tried to collect the dirty dishes and take them to the sink. She wanted to be useful, and she enjoyed washing dishes. She liked taking a cloth and wiping away anything that covered the pattern. Mother Reed's dishes weren't beautiful, but they deserved to be made clean again. Fumiko gently placed her bowl in the sink and walked toward the table. As she reached out her hand to collect Thomas's plate, Mother Reed pushed Fumiko's hand away with her elbow.

"Thomas, you and that girl better get to bed. We all have work to do tomorrow," she said, stacking Thomas's plate on top of her own. The couple left the kitchen in silence and followed his mother's instructions. Fumiko lay awake staring into the dark bedroom. Thomas reached for her hand in his sleep, but she slid her hand under her thigh.

When Fumiko awoke the next morning, she was in bed alone. Thomas had gone to see Mr. Myers, the owner and operator of the local IGA. The store had been open for almost two years now, and according to the letters his mother had written him while he was in Japan, business was booming. Prior to Thomas's arrival, his mother had spoken to Mr. Myers concerning a possible position at the store for her son. Mr. Myers assured Thomas's mother there would be an opening for him as a stocker as soon as he could get there. Thomas felt he could waste no time. The sooner he began working, the sooner he could save enough money for a house. Thomas crept out of their bedroom clothed in a crisp white shirt that his wife had packed neatly in his suitcase, a black tie, and brown trousers. He didn't want to wake Fumiko. Mother would be awake shortly, and he was sure her plans included a hefty day's work for his wife.

Thomas walked the two miles to the grocery, past the neighbors he'd once known so well. Their houses, silent and confined, perhaps because of the hour. At the stop sign, he turned left toward town, and in the quiet he began to think just how tough these times would be on his wife. He reassured himself with the idea their situation would only last for a short while, a year maybe two, and his wife was strong. He remembered their first few outings when she talked about her family. Her home had been burned to the ground with her mother still inside, the casualty of a firebomb. If she could withstand that pain, he was certain she could face living with his mother for a bit, but he'd lied to his wife about his mother. He'd known how she'd react. She'd told him in her return letter that Fumiko was not welcome in her home, but he'd made the decision to come.

"Lazy girl, get up. We have clothes to wash and mend, baking to do, and wood to chop. Did you think you were just going to lie in bed all day?" said Mother Reed.

Her voice was so loud that Fumiko was sure she was standing by her bed, but she wasn't. She was in the kitchen. Fumiko rummaged through her suitcases to find presentable clothing. She was looking for something respectful, but also something she could get dirty. She found what she needed. Brown slacks and a dark blue blouse should be suitable for wood chopping. She tucked in her shirttail as she walked to the kitchen.

"My, don't we think we're fancy? Well, I can tell you one thing, you're not going to prance around my house and yard all dressed up like you have money to spend," said Mother Reed.

Fumiko felt her throat close tight. She had sewn the blouse from scraps of leftover material, and the slacks had a tear. She had nothing else to wear.

"I will find something else to wear, Mother Reed."

"No need, girl. I have clothes for you. May be a little big, but it's better than walking around like you're sassy."

"Yes, thank you. I am very grateful," Fumiko said.

Mother Reed stomped from the kitchen, but soon returned with a heap of clothes in her arms. She threw them on the floor at Fumiko's feet.

"Put them on."

Fumiko gathered the clothes and turned to leave the kitchen.

"No, girl. I mean put them on now. You don't have a thing I've not seen before."

Fumiko looked at Mother Reed with pleading eyes. She could not be serious. They had just met the night before. She could not be expected to strip down to her undergarments.

"Come on. We don't have all day. Just get on with it. I got clothes to wash," she insisted. Still in disbelief, Fumiko stared at Mother Reed. She let one tear fall from her eye as she unbuttoned her slacks. As they fell to the floor, she grabbed at the pile of clothes at her feet.

"Don't you even know how to undress and dress yourself?" Mother Reed shouted, moving closer to Fumiko. "Take all of your clothes off then you put on a new set. Not one thing at a time.

Get that shirt off. Hurry up, now. I've been waiting on you too long as it is."

Fumiko stood in the cold kitchen in only her silk underpants as she began to unbutton her blouse.

"What in the world my boy sees in you I'll never know," she said as she walked out of the kitchen.

Fumiko bit her lip as she searched through the pile of clothes for pants to cover her shivering legs. The pants were at least three sizes too big. She rolled the waist of the pants over until they stayed put. She then grabbed the itchy wool shirt from the pile. Like the pants, the shirt was also too big, but she made it work. She rolled up the sleeves and tucked the bottom into the pants. These clothes smelled. They'd been Mother Reed's gardening and housecleaning clothes for the past week and hadn't been washed, but Fumiko stood as tall as she could in those clothes. She was ready to work.

As Fumiko walked onto the porch, she observed Mother Reed attending to the unkempt collie mix pulling at his chain, allowing him to slobber over her face as she scraped brown mush into his bowl. He slopped it, and she smiled, stroking his back as he ate. When he was finished, she rinsed the plate with the hose, and went inside. Not a word spoken between the women separated by a few feet.

Fumiko took hold of the ax and began to split the wood, hauling and stacking the broken pieces as she worked. As the afternoon replaced the morning, and the sun rose higher and hotter for the late spring day, she missed the incessant bark of the dog. It'd been comforting, consistent in a way. She walked toward his pen, the dugout of dark mud, and found him pulling and crying in a breathy grunt. The rusted pie plate that kept his water was spilled. The dog's eyes, wide and afraid, were not angry, and he lay down in the mud while she overturned his mistake.

The outside silence prompted Mother Reed to secure the safety of her dog and the success of her visitor. Through the screen door, she found Fumiko refilling the dish. He'd done it again, she reasoned. He wandered onto her front porch a month ago, thin and sick. Dead—she thought, until his skin twitched under her hand. She'd bathed him and fed him and kept him, for what she didn't know.

After hours of chopping, hauling, and stacking wood, Fumiko saw Thomas walking up the road to the house. She'd missed breakfast and lunch, and now it was time for dinner. She'd been so busy with the wood-pile she didn't notice the sun was setting and Mother Reed had gone inside. Thomas stared at Fumiko in disbelief. Her nose and cheeks had been burned by the heat of the sun, her already disgusting clothes were soaked with sweat and a little urine, and her hand had blisters on them the size of dimes.

"What in the world happened to you today? You look like you've been through the ringer," Thomas said.

Fumiko just stared into his dark blue eyes. She wanted to tell him everything. She wanted to tell him how she had been humiliated in the kitchen and forced to wear disgusting clothes too big for her body. She wanted to tell him that she had been outside chopping wood since nearly the time he left. She wanted to tell him that she had not been offered a bite to eat all day. She wanted to tell him that she had to drink water from the barrel by the house that she had to cup in her filthy hands. How, in the middle of all this, she was the one to tend to his mother's dog.

Fumiko wanted to tell her husband all of those things, but she was too exhausted to do anything other than gape at him.

"I got the job. It pays good, better than I expected," Thomas said, his hands in his pockets. "Mr. Myers promised me a raise after six months if I keep on doing a good job. He told me that he was trying to get enough men to volunteer so he could start a fire squad. I'm going to help him talk to some of the guys around town about joining up. And, I can keep any dented cans or banged up packages. Just think, you'll get to try all kinds of food you've never had before." He shifted his weight from one side to the other.

Fumiko tried to produce a little laugh, but she was too tired.

"Thomas, I thought I saw you walking up the road. Come in and wash up for dinner," Mother Reed called from inside the house.

"Just a minute, Mother," Thomas said as he walked to the bucket of water sitting by the shed. He motioned for Fumiko to follow him. She did, stumbling, her legs weak and unfamiliar.

They had no strength left in them. She'd stood over a woodpile for hours and couldn't be ordered to move at a whim. She shuffled to the side of the shed where Thomas was washing his face and hands. He'd had a good day, and she was happy for him. He was working for her, too. She needed to remember that.

When he was done, Thomas took Fumiko's hands and tenderly dipped them into the water. How it burned them. She wanted to scream, but she did not dare. She would not open her mouth in resistance. As her hands were soaking, Thomas took a rag from his pocket and dipped it into the water. He then wiped Fumiko's face with a soft sweep.

When he was done wiping her face and hands, he threw the rag back into the bucket. He gave her an innocent pat on the bottom, as was his custom, and they began to walk towards the house. She half-smiled at her husband and looked up to the sky to see the birth of the night's stars.

Mother Reed met the pair at the door. "Son," she said, "Check the garden shed. I think there's a pair of your father's old work gloves somewhere. Your wife will need them come tomorrow."

Thomas turned away from his wife, following his mother's instructions. This time Fumiko entered the house alone, her confidence earned in the day's labor. Mother Reed kept her back to her daughter-in-law, busying herself with unnecessary dinner preparations. In the bedroom, Fumiko sat on the edge of the bed, evaluating the damage to her hands. Raising her head, she saw on top of the chest of drawers a jar of salve someone had put there to heal her wounds.

Breath to Bones

A Novella

Mt. Laurel

Have you heard?

It's a shame.

Expect they'll have an open casket?

You ever seen one?

Better off dead than having something wrong with it.

Bridge is like to go crazy over this. Again.

I told you I seen them turkey buzzards flying the other day.

We heard Virginia almost fainted when she saw it. That woman's been through more than Job himself.

Jack

God damn you, God. I never said it before, but I reckon you'll for-give me for it this time. You're supposed to be good at that sort of thing.

How are we going to live now? A baby the size of a watermelon come out of Bridge's belly dead'r than a doornail. A little girl too—a sorry sight. Bridge pushed and cried till the end knowing all along weren't no joy going to come from it. I liked to lost my mind. Did you?

The nurse come in and said we could leave today. Said Bridge'd be better off resting in her own bed. Yanked out the needle in Bridge's hand, smacked a bandage on it, and grinned. Bridge never moved. "Sorry for your loss," the nurse said. Not tenderhearted though like she meant it. She was a curt woman with her thick neck and wide feet. Same one that yelled at Bridge when she was crying, trying to push out the baby after the doctor'd told her there weren't no heartbeat.

"You've got a job to do, miss," she'd said. "Baby's got to come out one way or another."

Now I'm supposed to put her in the truck and drive us home like everything's fine. Take her into the house with all the baby things she's been fussing over for months.

What day is it? Friday, no Saturday. I've missed two days of work and have to be out Monday, too. They got to understand. Need to keep the job to pay these damn hospital bills I know are coming.

"Wake up Bridge," I say. "Let's go on home." I pat her thigh through the blankets. I take her jeans and t-shirt from the back of the chair and squeeze them in one hand. I'm a fool, standing here staring at her. Prickles of red cover my face.

She smacks her tongue against the roof of her mouth. A week ago I'd hear the sound and wake up to get her a glass of water, but this time my feet don't move.

She blinks and squints, the light harsh. Her head rolls forward, and her eyes cut toward me.

What she's woke up into I can't tell.

Kate

A singlewide with a rusted-out roof on a rented lot and a dead baby—all she's got now. Bridge should've known better. Now look at her.

Turn if you're going to turn, moron. Want me to slam into the back of you to buy you a new car and a fur coat? Not today.

Mama made me hold the damn baby. I didn't want to, but she said I'd be sorry if I didn't. She was full and heavy with plenty of shiny blue-black hair. Blood red lips. A dead baby Snow White if there ever was such a thing.

Nobody wins an argument against Mama except Bridge. I guess I did one time—when she let Monroe Davis come pick me up in his rusted out black Camaro to take me to the movies. What a prize I won there. It was the same week daddy left, so she was too tired to put up much of a fight.

Yeah, I swerved, I know. Didn't hit you though did I? Keep walking. You're ok. You'll get home in time to watch Donahue like all the other old ladies.

Oh Hell, Mr. Williston is in tonight. Adding a spoiler to a Honda don't make it a racecar. He'll be over checking the eggs while I'm stacking the yogurt cups, inching his way over to me. "Just to help you out, sugar," he says. Maybe his wife'll come in tonight because he forgot the cat food for the hundredth time, and he'll hear her voice and drop a couple cartons. I'd like to see that again.

Damn. Where'd I put my gloves? My fingers are liable to break off if I don't start wearing them regular.

It was last summer—no, the summer before that. Some of us had spent the week after graduation at Myrtle Beach. I came back real tan, and he'd said something about it. That's what makes me remember.

My shift was nine to nine, but Ed, the old man who they hired to mop and wax the floors, called out. Mr. Williston asked if I could stay after the store closed and help him. I don't know why I didn't tell him to ask Sammy. He was working, and he's always wanting to work. He wants to move up in the company. He's told everybody.

Maybe I knew he was going to try and wanted him to—a little. We'd flirted some. He'd had the deli lady cook us some steaks one weekend while we were working, and we ate them in his office. I liked the special treatment. I can't lie. But he was married and kind of fat and I always knew I'd never go all the way with him.

I was finishing between the registers, and I was bent over the mop handle when he walked up to me.

"Nice bra," he said.

I stood up quick and straightened my shirt. "Thanks," I said, shoving the mop in the bucket.

"I'm done with my half of the floor. Looks like you need some help." He took a step toward me and tried to put his arm around my waist.

I moved to the side, bumping into the bucket. "I'm done. Just need to dump the water in the back." The bucket's wheels squeaked as I pushed it forward.

He stopped the bucket with toe of his boot. "Don't get shy on me now," he said.

"Give me a break," I said. I remember hoping he didn't notice the nervousness in my voice when I said that.

"Let's go out to my car."

"I need to go home. I'm tired. I worked late for you, remember."

"You owe me."

"I don't owe you a thing." I walked toward the door, but it didn't open. He'd locked us in to keep us safe.

"Open the door," I said.

"So now you want me? What do I get?" He walked to me and stopped so close we couldn't have been an inch apart.

I looked up at him. His spearmint breath drifted down onto my face. "Some other time," I said.

"I'm going to remember you said that," he said as he unlocked the door.

I walked out. I was slow and deliberate. Somewhere in between wanting him to know he hadn't scared me and wanting him to still want me later.

I see Sammy through the back glass. He comes in early to get the carts from the corrals. None of the managers notice.

Oh, man. He's coming over here. I can't even get one last minute for myself.

"Hey, Kate," he says, dangling a cigarette in his mouth while he talks.

"How's it going?" I say, stepping out of the car. "Let me get one of them."

He holds the lighter too close to my face.

"You got anything in your car for a squeaky door? Something's rubbing, and it's getting on my nerves." I exhale. My smoke tangles with his then disappears.

"Probably," he says, letting the butt fall from his mouth. "Mom dropped me off today, so she could drive my car to work. I'll let you know." He smashes the dying butt with one of the cart's wheels.

"Appreciate it," I say. "You ready to head in?"

"I guess," he says. "You're buddy's working tonight." He turns his head toward the Honda.

I inhale, crushing the filter between my lips then toss it on the oil-stained asphalt. "I got other things to worry about besides him."

Carl

Virginia's here. Hope she's not in there telling her damn Bible stories. I ain't in the mood. Probably what chased Rob off if the truth be told.

Grass needs a good mowing, what little there is of it. Me and Jack can take care of it. Keep us out of the house.

I find a spot of grass by the railing, just out of sight. I pull the faded leather flask from my shirt pocket. Need me a little swig before I go inside.

Sonofabitch. Couldn't have happened at a worse time—Jack just getting the new job and all. I hope Bridge has got more sense than to ask him to take more days off. There's not a thing you can do except work to keep food on the table and keep your head clear. Hell, if you ain't going to drink, you have to work. Don't let Virginia tell you any different. She'll try to run everything, but you're the man.

The screen door opens. It has to be Jack. He's the only one ever comes looking for me.

"I'm coming in," I say. I wipe my lips with the back of my hand and return the flask to my pocket.

"We knew you were here," Jack says. "Miss Virginia peeked at you through the curtain." He leans over the porch railing, resting his chin on his thick forearms.

"Sounds about right. Y'all have supper yet?"

"Bridge drank a grape cola," Jack says. "I'm having some chicken and dumplings one of them ladies brought over. Want some?"

"Is Virginia eating with us?"

"No. She's in the back telling Bridge goodbye," Jack says. "Said she was going over to the cemetery to look at the plot."

"Believe I will then."

Jack goes on in the house as I make my way up the steps. The cracked railing feels good in my palm. I rub my hand against the grain, hoping to draw in a splinter or two. Give me something to pick at later.

"Good evening Carl," Virginia says. The storm door swings wide almost smacking my nose.

"Virginia," I say. "Hope you're getting along all right." I keep my eyes focused on the tops of my boots.

"Just one thing after another as usual," she says. "Working on all the arrangements."

"Appreciate it," I say. I know what a woman like her wants to hear.

"See if you can get Jack to clean up the yard a little bit. They'll be having plenty of visitors, and it'd be a sign of respect to them," she says.

I throw my hand up at her as she slams herself inside the car. I watch her spin gravel as she escapes. Damn. I know nobody'd ever be good enough for my little girl if I'd had one, but we're not too bad. Hardworking, honest, and I'm about the only man I know of not to run out on his wife. Hell, it was her that left.

I open the door. A jumbo pack of baby wipes, still with its white bow on top, sits on the floor in the corner. The moist, creamy smell leaks from the package and mixes with the warmed chicken and dumplings. It makes me sick to my stomach.

Virginia

Gladys has the best flowers. Mr. Shire collects the body at noon. The little blue dress I bought will do fine. Kate can drop it off. Just a small service. The plot next to Papa Harold. I'll go look at in the morning.

Liquor on his breath. Think Carl'd have gotten over all that by now. I did. Never took one sip anybody knew of. Looks bad. Worn out at his age. Graduated high school a few years before me.

"One cheeseburger with mayonnaise, lettuce, and tomato only and a large sweet tea. That's all," I say into the gray box. Jack should've offered to pack me some supper to take with me. Heaven knows all I'm doing. He doesn't think like that. Probably never will.

He had the same look on his face at the hospital as he did the day they got married—scared to death. Rob had just finished reading him the riot act—as much as Rob could. I'd heard them on the way back from the bathroom. The men were dressing in the Adult Sunday School room. He told him things like "Bridge is so sensitive" and "She should be going to college" and "You have to be the one to look after her." If they hadn't been just on the other side of the door, I wouldn't have heard him. He barely spoke above a whisper. I don't think Jack said a word.

The girl at the drive-thru window has a terrible complexion. Red blisters cover her nose and cheeks. My stomach churns for a moment. I don't stop to count my change. I toss the bag into the seat and dig for the burger. The first bite is the best. I lick the cheese stuck to the wrapper and crumple it in my hand.

I've barely got the car door open and the phone is ringing. Who is it now? Another casserole delivery? When would be the best time for them to drop by to say they're sorry? What can they do to help? I don't know. There is no best time for any of it I want to say. I suppose it's better for them to ask me than to call on Bridge. I am the mother.

Before I can say hello, I hear her.

"Mama. Mama," she says. "Cabbage, Mama. She told me to use cabbage leaves. Get it for me, Mama. Please."

Kate

"Line three, Kate. Phone call on line three." It's Brenda, the nighttime booker, with her fizzy voice. We call her Velveeta behind her back because she always has a plastic grin smeared across her face. Nobody has that much to smile about.

"Dairy department, Kate."

"It's your mama. Are you busy?"

"No. About ready to leave. Why?"

"I need you to get a head of green cabbage to take over to your sister's before you come home."

"She needs cabbage now? It's nine o'clock at night. She can't be cooking."

"She called me a little bit ago and asked me to get it for her. Honestly, I'm too worn out. Can you please do this?"

"Fine. I'll take by on my way home. What the hell is it for?"

"Don't curse at your mama. All I know is she needs it tonight."

"All right."

"Drive careful," she says. I hang up the receiver before the goodbyes.

In the produce department I find a medium sized cabbage. A few brown curls around the edges of the leaves but good enough. I think about trying to sneak out with it. It's twenty-nine cents a pound. Who'd miss it? But there's no good way for me to hide it, so I pay my hard-earned money for a cabbage for a sister I barely talk to.

Jack left the door open for me. Seeing his feet hanging over the couch's edge, I try to be quiet coming in. He's awake though, watching a wrestling match.

"I spoke to your mama," he says. "I didn't know Bridge called her."

I don't know what to say, so I walk down the hall toward the bedroom.

Jack has a silly look on face as I walk past. Maybe he's waiting on some sort of instruction from me. What do I know about all of this?

Bridge is in her nightgown. Her body looks small and overwhelmed by the folds of the gown. She's propped the top half of her body on a pillow with her chin dropped and her shoulders hunched forward. The sickness in her head came through her body, and here she is looking the way I've imagined her all my life. Her eyes are locked on me, I think, or maybe something else.

"Here you go," I say. I think about slinging the thick head towards her and letting it roll up the quilt, but I catch myself. Instead, I shuffle between the empty crib and the side of the bed and offer it to her.

She takes hold, her cupped hands sagging under the weight. I smile but don't know why. I feel my eyes widen in a gesture of nervousness and confirmation. Ready to escape from this clumsy exchange, I turn toward the door.

"Granny Roxie," Bridge says. "Use it to dry up the milk you said. You know all the secrets." I glance over my shoulder. She's unbuttoned her gown and pulled two large cabbage leaves with bulging white veins and set them in front of her.

Our grandmother came back from the grave to talk to her? Figures. She's losing her mind again or maybe Granny did pay her a visit. Bridge has always been everybody's favorite.

I stare as she lifts her arm, tucking one leaf between breast and bra. The blue Sterman's Department Store tag dangles under her armpit. A gift from a member of Mama's congregation when they hosted the baby shower for her in the fellowship hall. We had warm cucumber and cream cheese sandwiches cut into triangles and foaming pineapple punch in a crystal bowl. I arrived late and didn't have the common decency not to wear blue jeans some woman said.

Bridge takes the second leaf, slips it in, and buttons the front of her gown. She exhales through her nose and relaxes into the mattress. I move close to her, not knowing if I should talk. Her eyes are closed. Her breaths shallow but sufficient.

I remove the cabbage from the bed, dropping it back into the plastic bag to save for later. I turn off the lamp on the nightstand, knocking over two pill bottles, but she doesn't move. She lies there half-asleep, waiting for her body to dry like you would fingernail polish.

I trade the cabbage for a beer and drink it on their porch listening to Jack snore and the chirps from a family of crickets under the steps.

Bridge

2:37 glowing Hell-red—an awful sight. My eyes ache, so they stay half-closed folding me into the dark. The leaves are warm and limp against my breasts. I drop them on the floor and rub my hand over an empty belly.

My lips are dry and cracked. I run my tongue over them and enjoy the sting. It's the voices that are loud. Men and women all around, the buzz of the refrigerator, the tick of Jack's alarm clock. No one can sleep here.

I pull my legs through the sheets and drop my feet on the floor. I rise and am steady. One long stride after the other delivers me to the front door. Like running bases playing softball. I was good once.

Jack is snoring. Of course you can sleep. I'll be fine. The lock is tricky, I know. I'll be quiet. There. See? You never moved.

I inhale. It's night air. Still with memories of its day but working to start new. Somewhere in the middle.

I sit in the wooden chair. I'd asked for a rocker. My head drops back, and through squinted eyes I see stars. Divide them by rows. Easy.

My toes and fingers tingle. I lick my lips again.

"Granny," I say. "I hear you. Yes. It helped. I'll put them in again. Where are you? I can't see you."

She came like I knew she would. She always took care of me.

"I count twenty-seven so far," I say, pointing up. "How many do you see?"

I lay my hands on the end of the armrests, palms facing up, waiting.

Jack

The kitchen clock says it's after seven. I smack my tongue against the roof of my mouth. It's the salty dough from those dumplings. Give most anything for my morning cigarette. No need to have quit smoking now. Still see the ashtray ring on the coffee table if I look hard enough.

I'll sweep off the porch then fix us a couple bowls of cereal. She might enjoy that. She used to. I'd make them on weekend mornings, and we'd lie in the bed eating cereal and watching cartoons like little kids.

Damnnation. She's sleeping in the porch chair. I touch her forehead with the back of my hand. It's cold—no telling how long she's been out here. Close to all night looks like. I should've gotten up and checked. I thought I heard you, but damn it, I'm tired too.

I drag the other porch chair close to her and slide into it. She doesn't move. A breeze pushes hair over her eyes, and she exhales one soft breath after the other. Pretty—even now out here in her nightgown, no bath and all. I lean sideways and kiss her temple. I feel my face flush warm, wanting another but stop myself.

I rise and step down off the porch. Cool dew moistens my bare feet. Damn these neighbors and their cigarette butts all over the yard. Least they could do is keep them on their own patch of property. Virginia'll want me to clean them up and mow the grass—for looks, she'll say. If any of her busybody friends had any sense, they'd know better than to expect a perfect place right now. Hell, we're not throwing a party.

I choose the ones with a little life left in them, blow off the dirt, and slip them into my pocket. A cola can rolls tink-tink-tink across the gravel drive.

I'll stay, *we'll stay*, right here until the sun burns off the morning fog.

Mt. Laurel Times

Obituaries

Cline, Holly Ann

Holly Ann, infant daughter of Jack and Bridget Cline of 12 Garnet Loop, died Thursday, June 15, 1995 at Mt. Laurel Memorial Hospital. Surviving in addition to her parents are maternal grandparents Rob and Virginia Evans and paternal grandfather Carl Cline.

The funeral service will be held at Harvest Faith Church on Monday, June 22 at 3 PM. The family will receive visitors in the fellowship hall following the service.

Shire Funeral Home is serving the Cline family.

Rob

I shouldn't have given her over to him. I had that feeling I some-times get. Something wasn't right. Bridge was too tender to be with him. Should've made her go off to the school she got into where she could've painted like she loved. Got a stack of those watercolors in the basement. Ginny never did want any part of them.

"Her art is what makes her sick," she said. The doctors at the hospital told her that.

"It's good to her," I said.

"No. She's crazy because of it. All the time alone locked in her bedroom. Not coming out for days not even for a sandwich or to brush her teeth. It's not good to stay inside your own mind for too long."

"It's a gift, her talent."

"Nothing is a gift that makes a person behave like she does."

What did any of us know? Turns out, nothing. Tried to kill herself even after we took her paints away.

Here I am reading my grandbaby's obituary getting black ink stains on my fingertips like everybody else who paid two quarters. I'd at least expected Kate to call me for a minute, but she's got her own business to tend to I suppose.

How's it going to look if I don't go to the service? What if I do? Who cares anyway? Half the people going will be there out of plain curiosity.

Ginny might still call. If she has time.

Maybe I should've given us another chance if I hadn't been so hard-headed. All done with now. People took the sides they were always going to take. Wouldn't have mattered what they knew.

I refold the newspaper, bend it in half, and tuck into the side table. I push hard on the volume button of the remote control, bringing the Duke's drawl into focus. Darn that Maureen O'Hara for looking so pretty on a day like this.

Mt. Laurel

Rob and Virginia? They didn't divorce?

Should've put Carl's wife's name in there somehow—it'd been nice if they'd named the baby after her.

Hope the service is short. Heard the pastor there likes the sound of his own voice.

Think I'll take make an apple-nut cake to take. You taking a sweet or a casserole?

The middle of the afternoon? Won't be easy taking off from work.

Virginia

I run my fingers over the few black dresses I have. This long one with the silk blouse will do fine. The neckline flatters me.

"Yes, thank you for coming. We do appreciate your thoughtfulness."

My voice is high. A slight smile. Show no teeth. I nod my head and offer my hand.

Chipped polish already. Need to repaint—Crushed Cherry will look the best.

"Terrible tragedy, I know. There aren't any good words."

Better this time. Lower eyes and shake head.

"Mrs. Woody, you didn't have to come out all this way. We would've understood." Place hand on her shoulder and give a gentle pat. Her son Raymond will be behind. Meet his eyes.

Flats? No, need the height. Go with the black patent leather heels.

I dig through scarves and gloves in the bottom drawer of chest. Finally—grandmother's embroidered yellow handkerchief.

"Couldn't have happened at a worse time. I know Bridge will be glad to know you came by."

Dab corners of eyes with handkerchief.

I set my hair in Velcro curlers, wrapping each section of hair tight as a tick around each cylinder.

All my tools are arranged on the bathroom sink: black eyeliner pencil, peach lip liner and matching lipstick, and cream blush.

"Kate," I yell, massaging moisturizer into my cheeks. "You need to start waking up."

Upward circles stimulate blood flow and help prevent wrinkles.

"I know you heard me," I say. "We're going to be busy today."

"What do you mean we?" Kate says. "What do I have to do?" Her bare feet smack the kitchen linoleum as she pounds into my bedroom.

A large grey Appalachian State sweatshirt, not her own, serves as a nightgown. Brown curls shade her eyes. As she leans against the bathroom door, she has no idea what a natural beauty she is. So different than me and Bridge.

"Have you talked to your daddy?"

"Not lately."

"I need you to go over there and tell him what all is going on. He might already know, but it'd be nice if you saw him."

"You mean Jack hasn't talked to him? I know Bridge is wacked out of her mind, but you'd think Jack would have."

"I don't think so, or we would've have heard from him by now. Tell him to be at the church at a quarter past two."

"I don't feel like talking to him about this. Can't you call him this one time? It's about your own child for Christ's sake." Her brow is tight and her voice gritty.

"I asked you to do it, and watch your mouth."

"What else?" She shifts her weight, crossing her arms.

"The baby's blue dress is hanging on my closet door. Take it to Mr. Shire this afternoon. It's what she's going to wear."

"Fine. You going to church?"

"No. Are you?" She doesn't flinch. Her eyes meet mine.

"Then why is all this makeup and stuff laid out?"

"One less thing I'll have to do tomorrow."

She shuffles into the hallway, and I hear her bedroom door slam. She'll crawl back into bed until the last minute like she always does. I should've asked her what she was planning to wear tomorrow, but that might've been too much. If nothing else, she can wear something of mine. Slip right into anything, and it'll look like it was made for her.

Kate

Daddy's and the funeral home—fuck me. I bury my face in the pillow. I'd tried to go back to sleep, but she kept slamming her bathroom drawers closed on purpose I'm sure. She doesn't even care I have to work this afternoon. Everything has to be done her way on her schedule. So what if I didn't jump at the chance to get dressed and out of the door like she did. It'll get done. I'll go over to Daddy's and sit through half an hour of throbbing silence interrupted by prickles of questions I don't want to answer. Then I'll drive to the funeral home to hand deliver a dress that'd fit one of my old Cabbage Patch dolls. I'll do what I'm supposed to because I can't get away with *not* doing it. I'm no Bridge.

Did we have fun? I chew on my thumbnail, thinking it over. I guess we did have some good times together—back when we were little and before she started going crazy, and I smartened up. But we were always so different. She was the one they worried about. Never me. They knew I'd always be able to take care of myself. I have, and I did. They'd be surprised to know just how much.

She might try again, they'd say. So what if she did? I never wished anything bad on her, but she made our lives miserable.

There was the time Granny Roxie took us to Tweetsie Railroad. I was eight and Bridge was ten. That was the best time the three of us ever had together.

Granny Roxie picked us up early in the morning. Bridge and I shared Daddy's old army duffle bag. Mama'd packed our clothes in tight and told Bridge to take them out and hang them up as soon as we got to the motel, so we wouldn't look like street urchins everywhere we went.

Bridge sat up front, and I sprawled across the back seat with my comic books. Granny let Bridge change the radio stations as much as she wanted. Just when she came across a song she knew I liked, she'd change it. We ate toast and strawberry jelly for breakfast we'd fixed ourselves, so it was fine with us when Granny said she wanted to find a "pretty" spot to eat our lunch. She drove till there was a rest stop with a picnic table in the grass where we had soggy tomato and mayonnaise sandwiches and potato chips. For a minute, we ate and laughed and were the same.

We spent all afternoon at the park, riding the roller coaster and the train, and we split two cotton candies and a funnel cake. When we got to the motel the neatest part was how Granny'd let me walk down the hall by myself to fill our ice bucket. She'd also given me fifty cents to buy a Coke from the vending machine as long as I promised to share it with Bridge.

Bridge and I fell asleep in one of the double beds, but the next morning Bridge was curled up next to Granny in her bed. I watched them for a while—before Granny woke up and went in the bathroom to curl her hair. They laid there facing each other, their breaths in rhythm, Granny's arm curled over Bridge's waist. They were the sisters me and Bridge should have been.

Rob

"Come on in the house," I say, holding the screen door open for her. She doesn't catch my smile because she walks with her head down.

She stands by the couch and runs her finger along the cushion's crease. She shuffles her weight from one foot to the other before taking a seat.

"I was watching some TV," I tell her. "Remember when we'd get pizza on Friday nights, and it was our turn to choose the movie? Man, your mama and Bridge hated those cowboy movies we picked."

Her response is a quick exhale through the nose. I thought she'd like to know I remembered.

"Daddy, I just came by to tell you Bridge—"

"Lost the baby," I interrupt as I stumble into the recliner.

"Yeah," she says, taking a bite out of her thumbnail.

"I read the obituary in the paper this morning." I try not to sound hurt but fail.

"I had to work," she says, her voice quick and high. "I thought maybe Jack would've called."

I reach for the remote control. "It's ok."

"Leave it on," she says, staring at the television.

"Bridge holding up?" I ask.

"I guess. She's home. Not really talking though."

"Your mama's doing all right, I'm sure."

"Yeah. Making all the arrangements, you know."

"She's the right one for all that."

"Yeah."

She's done talking, so I turn the volume up with the remote and sit back in the recliner. How often I've wished to watch one of these old movies with her. It's right funny how things happen.

Carl

I pull the rest of the piece out of the inside knuckle. Damned if I didn't get me a good splinter off Jack's railing. Suppose I'd better give him a call this morning. See if he needs help with anything. I pull the rotary toward me. That cordless phone Jack and Bridge give me for Christmas last year is still in the hall closet. Can't bring myself to use it. I like putting my finger in the wheel and watching it return home after each number. I appreciate hard work.

"Hello," Jack says. His voice is hoarse.

"It's me," I say. "You sick?"

"Tired."

"Want me to come over there and help you today?"

"That's ok. Just need to do a little bit of cleaning up outside."

"Well, I can come if you want company."

"Come on then. Like I said, I ain't planning to do too much, but you can go with me to take a load of trash to the dump."

"All right then. Be over in a minute."

We never have been the kind who say goodbye at the end of a telephone call.

Virginia

Anybody with any sense will see the grass has a fine emerald tint even if it does need mowed. She'll fit nice between all our mamas and daddies.

Lord knows it'd have to be that damn Vera Bern walking up here now. And with her cat no less. Takes the thing everywhere, screeching and whining. Liked to drove Bonnie crazy last week at the beauty shop. Singed my hair with the curling iron for the first time in years.

"I thought that was your car," she says.

"Just came by for a look before tomorrow," I say.

"Awful to have happen to anybody, I know, but especially Bridge," she says. "With all her trouble. Lord, have mercy. How in the world will she make it through this?" She kneads the cat's neck with her thumb, trying to keep him calm.

I ignore her question and take a deep breath. "How was the service this morning?" I ask. No telling who knows what or what's been said. More news is spread on Sunday mornings at church than by all the cable television channels combined—most all started by a poke and prod from Vera.

"Fine. Fine. Same as always. Dennis added you all to the prayer list, but most of us knew anyway," she says. "Sarah Morris's daughter-in-law is a nurse, you know."

No better story to share than death or divorce or when somebody thin gets fat.

"Let me know if there's even the least little thing I can do. We'll be seeing you tomorrow," she says. "I hope you're up for my coconut dream cake. It takes four hours to make, you know. It's the least I can do." Her cat releases a spine shivering scream then yawns.

She reaches out to pet my hand before charging through the parking lot bobbing her head like a chicken—running through the conversation again figuring what to tell people I should've said but didn't and how I looked when I did talk.

Who's she to come back here and interrupt my mourning? I don't have to be on till tomorrow. Lord knows I've spent my life trying to look the right way and say the right thing and do the right thing, always. But it's damn hard, and some days I can't keep up.

Kate

I throw my hand up—half waving back. I don't know if you can see me or not, but I see you. Still trying to be same dad you were when I was little. I glance in the rearview mirror before backing down the driveway. But it's been so long now, and I'm grown enough—I can see it in my eyes.

Why did you have to say Bridge "lost" the baby? Hell, she's not missing like Bridge left her at the mall or something. She's her mama for God's sake. She didn't do anything or not do anything to cause it. It just happened like a lot of things do. Not that you'd know. You stopped trying to know me when I was thirteen. If you really knew me, it'd kill you.

Now it's raining, and my wipers are busted—figures. At least it's not far from the funeral home to work. I'd never tell, but I'm glad to be working today. Keeps Mama off my case and gives me an excuse to stay away from Bridge. I don't know if she expects me to be at the trailer or not. I mean, she's not in her right mind, but it seems like sisters ought to help each other out. Well, I'm not going to feel guilty about it. I took the cabbage didn't I? There's nothing else I can do that'd make any difference.

At least there's no other cars in the lot except for a couple hearses parked under the overhang. I push open the door with my foot and grab the bag with baby clothes. The squeal from the hinge is getting worse. Hope Sammy is working tonight and brings me grease or something. I know he likes me. He's nice enough, but I can't look past his buckteeth, and most of the time his breath would gag a maggot.

I push the heavy oak door, and a burst of cold air crashes into me. I step through the lobby waiting to hear a voice or footsteps, but neither comes. Down the hall is a room filled with rows of caskets. It won't hurt to take a look.

There's an extra long one with white lining and large lace pillow—must be for a big man. The black one with the white lining is nice but no pillow. The brass buckles and handles must be standard on all the models. Some are half-open. Some are open all the way. It's like being in the showroom of a car dealership. I don't see any real small ones. Wonder if they had to get one in from another funeral home like in a trade or something?

"Good morning. May I help you?" It's Mr. Shire, the funeral home director. He looks at me like he's never seen me before, but his youngest boy Luke and I went to the same elementary school. He ran the cotton candy machine at the school fair on the last day and gave me a double swirl of blue on my paper cone.

"I'm Kate Evans. I'm here to—"

"Your mother, bless her, called me to let me know you were coming. She made all the arrangements on her way home from the hospital the day the poor thing died. Picked out the Rose Collection casket right away. That woman has the strength of Job."

"That's what she tells me." I hand him the bag and turn to leave.

"We'll have everything perfect for tomorrow. Don't any of you worry about the least little thing."

Not knowing what to say, I don't speak. I make some sort of sound and nod though I don't know if he noticed or not.

It's raining even harder now, and it's warmer. I splash through the empty lot to the car. The windows are fogged over. Is it on the inside or outside? I can never tell. I grab the ratty beach towel from the backseat and wipe the inside of the windshield. It's clear for a few seconds then becomes cloudy again. I turn on the wipers—tick, tick, tick. One surges across the windshield while the other doesn't move.

Virginia

He decided to take my advice. Thank heavens. And Carl here helping no less. One of those people who come around for a wedding or a new baby or death. In this case, he's hitting two birds with one stone.

Maybe I shouldn't think that way, but we don't see him. He's invited to my house to eat for Christmas Eve dinner and hasn't shown his face once. Bridge says he tells her he doesn't want to impose. When they exchange gifts, she and Jack have to go to his place, and they don't stay more than twenty minutes if that. He puts out one bottle of sparkling cider, and when it's gone, time's up.

"Virginia," Carl says. He nods at me then gives the rake a hard pull, collecting wet leaves and gravel in a heap.

I smile as I walk past him toward Jack who's hammering in a loose nail on the porch.

"Did she sleep last night?" I ask. He marks a final blow with the hammer before running the back of his hand across his forehead to catch a bead of sweat.

"Not much." His voice is curt. Not cold—curt. He sits the hammer on the railing and moves close to Carl.

Surely he's not mad at me. I've done nothing but try to help.

"Well, you're doing a nice job out here. I'll go inside and straighten up," I say. Who knows if they heard me. Carl's stuffing his pile of trash into the large black bag Jack's holding open for him.

The stale air inside the trailer hits me in the face. Jack's had the windows open, but that's just let in moisture and stink from outside. I crank up the window unit in the corner—nice cold clean air.

The kitchen sink is full of dishes. I guess I'll have to do them, too. Not a washrag or dry dishtowel in sight either.

I call for Bridge loud enough she can hear me. I doubt she's asleep anyway.

I walk down the hall and tap on her door. It's cracked, so I push it open the rest of the way. She's still in her nightgown, the crinkled edge of a cabbage leaf peaking above the neckline. I always thought that to be an old wives' tale. Never known anybody to use them.

At least she's up. I mean she's awake and sitting on the edge of the bed. It has to be better for her to be moving around than wallowing under the covers in this sour room another day.

"We need to look through your clothes and see if you've got something to wear." If she understands what I'm saying, I can't tell.

The closet door slides off the track when I touch the knob. Something else Jack needs to fix.

The space is divided in half. Hers on the right—pink blouses, a few pairs of slacks, a rock band t-shirt from a concert, and two dresses. The red wool sweater dress won't do, so it'll have to be the navy linen. It's dark enough to pass for this occasion. Goodness knows I can't take her shopping.

"What do you think about this?" I hold the dress in front of her, forcing a grin to show my approval.

She reaches for the hem, rubbing her thumb along the stitching, which I take as a yes, Mama, this is fine.

I hate to have her try it on, but we need to know it fits, and I need to know what it shows.

"Here, Bridge. Stand up for me, and let me see how it looks," I tell her. My voice jerks. "You can leave the gown on. It's thin enough to act like a slip."

I cup my hand on her elbow, and her fingers collapse around my forearm. My poor Bridge.

I pull the dress over her head like when she was a little girl, and we played peek-a-boo to keep her from getting scared while her face was covered. I work her arms into the sleeves and pull down, smoothing the coarse linen over her hips. She never twitches or stumbles. She's a large doll, waiting.

Carl

It's hard—just living, I mean. Work and children and never enough money to make things easy. Then there are the deaths. Mama and Daddy, a brother or sister in there somewhere, then your own damn wife or child. How we manage to put one foot on the floor in the morning is a miracle.

Son, I'll never say it to your face, but be glad you didn't get to know the baby. Be thankful you didn't wake up to her every day for years, hear her sweet voice even when she was yelling, and look into her eyes. I mean, your mama's eyes sparkled. People say that, and you hear it and think they're crazy. I can tell you, though, that woman's soul poured right out of her eyes into your own without you having to do a thing.

We buried her in the fall. Right after Thanksgiving. Do you remember? I did all the cooking because those damn ladies said they wanted to help but all they really wanted to do was come over and see what your mama looked like. How much weight she'd lost and how her hair had thinned. She couldn't have stood that, and I wouldn't let them ruin her any more than she already was.

She sat at the table with us, trying to smile and eat, all the while that damn fork bouncing all over her plate because her hand wouldn't stop trembling. I hate to hear the sound even now—the *clink, clink, clink*. You can't explain that to anybody, though. Not in any real way that'd make sense. After all, it's just a fork. Each *clink* was her moving away from me to a place I wasn't invited.

Clink. "I'm tired, Carl."

Clink, Clink. "This is our last meal together."

Clink, Clink, Clink. "I'm going to die and leave you here."

Jack

"Here," Virginia says. She waves a bulging white envelope in my face.

"You'll want these," she says. "Bridge will want these. Not now, maybe, but she will later on when she wants to remember." I don't say a word, and she takes off out the door.

What am I supposed to do with these pictures? She was snapping and snapping, and they were falling out all over the hospital floor, and she was picking them up and flapping them around trying to get them to develop.

Maybe Bridge will want to see. Maybe she'll put them in a photo album with our little girl's name on the front. Maybe she'll ask me to help her, and I will. Maybe she'll cry a little, and I'll put my arm around her. I might cry with her. Me and her sitting on our bed, pictures spread out, and us remembering, together, that day and this little girl.

When she's sleeping, when she's really deep-breathing asleep, I'll stick it in her jewelry box. Where, if she opens it up and sees the envelope, she thinks it's meant to be that she takes a look and remembers. Maybe.

Kate

Mama said, "Pants? Over my dead body," and we have one of those already, so it'll have to be the black denim dress.

You should've told me how much more there was to it than "sperm meets egg" like they taught us in health class. It all seemed so scientific—based on time and situation. Something I could control by not thinking about the probability at all.

Bridge was a mess and you'd run Daddy off by then. Not that I expected him to talk about sex. God, he can hardly open his mouth to mention the weather.

You get half the blame. For letting me go when you should've said no and for making me feel like I couldn't come to you after. Like *I'd* be the disappointment, the embarrassment—even when you had Bridge.

Any other time, you would've laughed in my face if I'd come begging you to let me go to the movies with a senior. But not this time. You waved me away. *Dallas* was on.

I'd called him back and told him I could go. Heard him grinning through the phone, I swear. I was one of the cool girls, riding in his dad's Camaro with the windows rolled down. Even though both fenders were rusted, I was proud when strangers looked over at us at stoplights.

He bought us a popcorn tub, which wasn't cheap, and we split an orange drink. When I took my first sip after him, a tingle ran all over my body. He was sharing himself with me. He took my hand from my lap and placed it in his, smoothing the skin with his fingertips.

When he reached over and unbuttoned my jeans, I was surprised but not afraid. Even when he climbed on top of me with his jeans lowered to his thighs, I felt warm and ready.

For a while, I was exactly what somebody wanted.

After the credits ended and the screen went black, somebody cut on the light, and he jumped off me, pulling up his jeans and yelling at me to hurry.

He dragged me by the arm through the fire exit door. No alarm sounded like I thought it would.

He didn't open the car door for me like he did when he picked me up, and the radio was blaring country music so loud I couldn't say anything if I'd wanted to.

When we pulled in the driveway, he reached into the backseat without looking, grabbed a sweatshirt and handed it to me.

"Root for the Mountaineers," he said. "I'm headed to Appalachian State next year."

I only had half the money for it. I took the rest from Bridge. She was back in the hospital, so she wouldn't be needing it anytime soon. Christy's cousin told me about the place and gave me a ride. I wore the sweatshirt he gave me and jean shorts. There was a blue vase with fake yellow flowers on a coffee table in the waiting room. The man, a doctor I guess, said everything went fine.

I cup my hand over a full belly—full of stillness and silence. A little sadness, but not regret. Never regret.

I think it fits okay. It's snug in the hips, but it's better than nothing. Really, I do mean nothing. It's the only dress I own. What do I even have this for anyway?

There—last snap of the band and hair is up. It's too warm to leave it down, and it's the last thing I want to have fight today.

I grab my makeup pouch from the dresser and rest it against my knee on the bed. Where is that tube of mascara? I dump the contents on the comforter. Here it is. Now the compact mirror. A little black cement on these lashes, and I'm all set. Maybe a finishing touch of nude lip gloss.

Graduation. That's it. All the girls were supposed to wear white knee-length dresses, but I couldn't find one I liked. I tried. Went to two different stores. The fit they threw about that at the lineup. Mama too, once she found out. But like I asked them, what difference did it make? The gown covered it up, so who'd know?

Brown heels. Oh, Mama'll love this. Shoes don't match the dress, heaven forbid! I jam the pile of shoes on the closet floor, poking them this way and that, but the door still doesn't want to close. It's the corner of the egg crate that's caught. On the top is the scarf box. Haven't looked at this in a while.

Granny Roxie's gift for my thirteenth birthday. It was folded into a perfect triangle so one full blackbird showed when I peeled open the tissue paper. I'd groaned at the time, telling her I'd never wear a scarf—it wasn't me. She'd insisted I'd grow into it.

There were many times I sat with it on my bedroom floor, smoothing it to its full square, and tracing my index finger over each silhouette. Beak to black breast to claw. Their midair flight across a sky of white silk.

If could just get this tied on right it'd help. I fold and crease, unfold and smooth, and bring it around my neck. The mirror's reversals offer little help. No bird has a head, now only feet show—a bead of sweat drops into a crease. What the Hell am I doing? I pull the silk tight, enjoying the punishment for my own inadequacy, then release.

I reach for the yellow beaded necklace bought with my own money for some forgotten event. At least it hides the red streak.

I fold the scarf to fit its box, aiming to expose a blackbird inside a crisp triangle, but fail—again.

I'll never be that kind of woman.

Jack

"Hello there, Jack," Rob says and pats me on the back. "Been a while." I nod, and open my mouth to say something but nothing comes out. He must've realized I was in a jam, so he half-smiles and moves on to Bridge. He tells her he's glad to see her, even now, and how sorry he is. She never looks at him. She keeps her eyes focused on the wall in the back. Maybe she's reading the board with last week's numbers: Sunday School Attendance: 54, Worship: 120, Offering: $800, but I doubt it. He leans down and kisses her cheek. She don't flinch.

Nobody pays him much attention. I know him and Virginia don't really get along, and Kate can be tough for anybody, but I don't know why him and Bridge aren't close. He was always decent to me. Treated me nice. Maybe he knew Virginia would give me a hard time enough for both of them.

I know he always thought Bridge should've gone to college. He told me that the day of our wedding. But he wasn't mean about it. It was like he felt sorry for me. Like maybe I didn't know what I was getting into with her and all—all her troubles when she was younger. I think he was looking out for both of us, really.

She'd told me about some of it, though. About feeling so lonely even before Rob and Virginia split up. A deep hole of lonely where she said she fell into and didn't really want out of—until she did.

The first time she tried, she slit her wrists. Rob found her and wrapped her up. She spent three months in a psychiatric hospital after that. Family could visit on weekends, and hers did, even Kate.

She's never mentioned the second time, and I haven't asked. Maybe I'm afraid of what she might tell me.

It was, *is*, something about her. Even knowing all of that and how her family is and mine. Like we were going to be different. I could make her happy like she made me. Like the times when I'd get home from work, tired as dog, dying to drop on the couch and put my feet up, she'd meet me at the door, tape player blaring, and we'd dance across the living room of the trailer. She'd knock something over, or I would, and we'd look down at it for a second then keep on moving.

She was the one who wanted a baby. I know everybody thinks it's my fault, but I told her I thought we should wait. Wait for a bigger house with a yard, wait for a better job for me, wait so we'd have more money— just wait. She said now was the time. She could feel it she said. She wasn't working, so she could stay home. Virginia wasn't too old, so she could help if we needed her. I wouldn't have to worry about a thing she said. She was ready.

We weren't ready. Not for this.

She's not ready.

Bridge

You said, "Look after Kate."

You said, "I love this one here—the horses pulling the carriage and the driver in the top hat. Let's hang it in the living room."

You said, "Bridget, come on out now. Supper's on the table."

You said, "Why did you do this? What made you do this?"

You said, "Your mama and I will be back for a visit in no time."

You said, "He's a nice enough boy."

You said, "I can't stand seeing you lying here—strapped to the bed like some animal."

You said, "You can turn around right now. Leave if you want. Me and your mama will take care of the guests and the food and the gifts."

You never said, "I'm sorry."

You think you found me. I found you first. Found you naked. In the bed. Lying in your own shit. I called Mama. Mama wasn't there. I whispered "Daddy." You didn't hear. You were dead.

Mama drank. You didn't. Then you did, and you were dead in the bed. You never saw me. I saw you first. You were mad you found me. I was mad you found me. I wanted to die. You wanted to die. We didn't. We found each other. In brown shit. In red blood. We woke up.

Virginia

Bridge and Jack in old folding chairs beside the casket. Family doesn't normally sit in the receiving line, but those two don't look like they'd last more than ten minutes on their feet. None of this is normal. Visitation and funeral in the same day. I mean it's just not done. All I can do is I hope everybody understands it's for Bridge's sake. The rest of us will stand.

Twenty minutes to show time.

"Carl." I wave him over. "You're by Jack."

How could he not wear an overcoat? A shirt full of wrinkles no less. He should've taken it to the cleaners if he couldn't press it himself. What'll people think? Bridge and Jack lost a baby, live in a trailer park, and the father-in-law looks like a street urchin.

"Rob." I tap him on the shoulder. "You're next to me." He shuffles forward. Loafers buffed to a solid shine. His eyes meet mine, begging for direction, consolation, maybe something more.

"Kate, you come over here by your daddy." The dress is too tight. Typical. I wish she'd at least try.

Ten minutes to show time.

I step out of place for a final look. Could be worse, I suppose. Jack has one hand resting on top of the casket—they kept it closed after all—and the other around Bridge's shoulder. They'll make it. Plenty of people make it through worse things than this. It is a shame though. I was looking forward to tea parties and dress up. A little one pulling at me saying "Granny." That'll have to wait. Who knows? It might even be Kate who—

The curtain goes up.

The Griffiths and the Martins—always dressed to kill. Gregory Griffith flies to New York City for a haircut once a month, and Sharon shops at all the nicest "boutiques" there. Rose Martin had some work done to her face even though she swears jogging tightened her neck and got rid of the crow's feet. Jogging around the world wouldn't have helped her any. Everybody knows Harold wears a hairpiece. Paid hundreds of dollars for it somebody said, and it floats a quarter inch above his head.

"So nice to see you and Rob together even under these circumstances," Sharon says. She doesn't shake my hand. She holds it and pats the back. I hate that.

I smile a stupid half-grin. It feels awkward, so I know it doesn't look right. I didn't know what to say.

She and Gregory move on to Rob. His smile is broad and flashy. He doesn't know what to say to them either.

The Martins file through without much excitement except Rose hugged Bridge and Bridge sat there like a lump on a stump. I can't fix everything.

"Mrs. Daniels." I catch the trembling, skeletal hand offered me. She smiles, a front tooth is missing. "Thank you so much for coming."

My nose and lips twitch. Damn the smell of mothballs.

Jack

The turkey was no good anyway. Ladies offered to bring us Thanksgiving dinner, but he wouldn't have it. He sat Mama on a stool with her back leaned against the counter while he mixed and chopped then scalded the gravy and burnt the bird. She'd tried to help, whispering what to put in the sweet potato casserole and how to cover the rolls so they wouldn't burn, but I don't think he heard a word she said. He kept on pulling pots and pans and glass dishes from the cabinets, clanging them together, searching for what I don't know. At twelve, I knew better than to ask.

The wind howled fierce at her service. A short deal, graveside only, at the church she grew up in. Where she took me, too, when we went to visit Mamaw.

I don't think there were twenty people there—must've been cause of the weather. I stood next to Daddy, watching him out of the corner of my eye. He never cried, so I didn't either. He stood there with his head down and shoulders rounded. His arms hung on his body like somebody was trying to pull them out of the sockets. When everything was over, he tripped in a little sunken spot in the grass walking back to the car. He was pitiful.

He will wipe away every tear from their eyes, and death shall be no more, neither shall there be mourning nor crying nor pain any more, for the former things have passed away.

None of us lives to himself, and none of us dies to himself. If we live, we live to the Lord, and if we die, we die to the Lord; so then, whether we live or whether we die, we are the Lord's. This is what the Sovereign Lord says to these bones: I will make breath enter you, and you will come to life.

Pretty much the same words. Old man with a coat and tie—all preachers are the same. Why not? Death is the same no matter who it happens to. There's only so much you can say about it. God and Jesus and coming home or going home, whichever it is.

I roll the cuffs of my sleeves to the elbow and stretch my legs. I guess the comfort's in the sameness of it all.

Bridge

I tried to go before you. I wanted to leave. I never wanted to be left. Take me with you where you are. Come back for me.

Kate

After church on Sundays, me and Jenny would play hide and seek in the cemetery. To this day, it's the best place to play. We'd crouch behind old gray headstones, some crumbling and worn clean of names and dates. The maples, one at the front of the cemetery and one in the middle, made pretty good spots, too. It was between that one, the middle with the spider-legged branch, and the fading Cox headstone where Kevin Thomas showed us his peter.

He visited his aunt one Sunday a month, and sometimes we'd let him play with us. He was thin and shy, light brown hair and glasses, and picked his nose right after snack in Sunday school. Once, Mrs. Marshall asked him if he knew the first four books of the New Testament, and he buried his head in his arms on the table and cried.

If he'd ever told anybody the story, he'd have sworn it was us who'd made him do it. Just as well though. Nobody would've believed me or Jenny anyway. Her grandmother brought her to church because her parents were "on something," meaning she was doomed from the start. I was the one who burped during communion prayer, meaning I'd be forever lacking common decency.

Yes, it was more likely he'd been forced to do it because we wouldn't allow him to play with us otherwise.

"You want to see something?" he'd asked. We were seated cross-legged with our backs to the tree. Neither of us wanted to say yes, but not knowing how to say no, we nodded. He unzipped his fly and with one finger, dug around in his white underwear until he flipped it though the opening.

I fell backwards against the tree while Jenny leaned forward with her hand stretched out like she wanted to touch it. Then quick as he flipped it out, he tucked his boyhood back in.

We laughed and smiled at one another. I gave Kevin a shove on his shoulder, and Jenny hid behind the tree, counting. We ran and hid, took turns between the roles of hider and seeker. Every once in a while, we'd collapse on the ground, green grass sprouting between our fingers as we rested. We tilted our heads back and played guessing games about the shapes of the clouds until they moved too far out of sight.

Jenny's grandmother brought her to church a few more times, but then she stopped coming with her. Maybe she moved.

In the fifth grade, Kevin hanged himself from a beam in his basement. His aunt added his parents to the prayer list during service.

I wonder if Jenny ever heard about Kevin?

Virginia

I'm being punished. All my kids are being punished. That has to be it. Dave showing up today. I know he came to see me. He was, is, a nice boy— man. God, help me. I can't hardly stand it. Bridge sitting over here like she's in a coma. Rob in the corner, smiling and eating like a court jester or something. Jack hasn't hardly held his head up. Kate—where is she now? Smoking somewhere no doubt. The stories that'll be told about us today.

And to top it all off, Vera over there standing behind her cake like she's waiting for somebody to come by and pin a blue ribbon on it.

The fellowship hall is full. Men and women and more children than necessary under the circumstances move in between and around each other in search of conversation and food. The condolences, the "I can't even imagine what you all are going through(s)" spoken over scoops of casseroles, after gulps of sweet tea and coffee.

It's not as though I don't appreciate it, the fact they came. Most all of them are good people in their own right.

Two ladies—I don't even know their names—attend to the buffet. Stacking and restacking finger sandwiches, removing crumbs, filling drinks. They seem kind.

A tiny old man, Mr. Levi, takes me by the elbow as he tells me how pretty he thought the flowers were. He stutters a bit and his coffee cup shakes in his hand. When he asks would I mind if he took a blue hydrangea bloom to Mrs. Levi, "She's been put in a home, you know," I smile and nod. I welcome him to anything we have. "Take her some food. We have plenty." Take whatever you want, but please move away from me before your coffee spills everywhere. He smiles and waves and stumbles toward the sandwiches.

"Excuse me for a minute," I say to no one in particular.

I make my way to the ladies' room upstairs. Please, Lord, let it be empty. What a relief to hear the stall door close and lock, protecting me for a few minutes. I stare at the rolled down pantyhose binding my knees. I slide my feet from my shoes. The tile floor cools my toes. Dave, Dave, Dave. Why in the world did you come here now? For this? God, I haven't thought about you—us—in forever.

You were home from college for the summer, and your mother brought you in to open a savings account. Your blue eyes sparkled like marbles. It was two, no, three Fridays before I got the nerve to ask you. I don't know why I was so nervous. I knew you'd come. I was attractive then.

The first time was the weekend the girls went to Tweetsie and Rob was fishing in Florida. Then there were church camping trips where Rob had to go to help the girls, the weekend I said I was with Aunt Blanche cleaning her basement, and the ladies' getaway weekend to Savannah. My heart's about to pound out of my chest thinking about it all.

I fizzled out. It wasn't you. You were as sweet as ever. Three months together. How exciting it was when you opened the motel room door to a queen-size bed just for us. We laughed and smoked cigarettes and drank vodka lemonades in between.

Brought me those pink tulips once. Said you loved me. I wasn't in it for that though. I already had too many to love. That's awful to say isn't it? Inside a church and at my granddaughter's funeral. Saying there were too many people in my life? Well, it's how I felt. I tried explaining it to you, but you didn't understand. You couldn't have.

The last morning I left you there. I didn't bring you a doughnut and a coffee when you woke up, and I stopped writing invitations on the backs of deposit slips. I counted your money to you in tens and twenties without ever looking up until you finally moved your account. I did miss you for a while.

Voices and heels burst through the door. I'm not sure which came first.

"Did you smell what Clara Daniels has on?" a woman says.

I peek under the stall. Tan pantyhosed calves with low brown heels and naked calves in high heels, the color of black grapes.

"Oh, be nice. You know her grandson killed himself last year. Jumped off a bridge somewhere over in Tennessee," another woman says. This voice sounds younger, probably the one without the pantyhose.

"I know, I know. All I'm saying is you'd think she'd have sense enough to air out something before wearing it. I hate the smell of mothballs."

"Just go on and use the bathroom would you so we can get out of here. They're sales in town I want to get to. I'm taking full advantage of the day I took off."

"And you're talking about me? What about you? For goodness sakes you're leaving a baby's funeral to go shopping."

I cough and rattle the toilet paper holder so they have no choice but to notice they're not alone. I can't stand people who don't pay any attention to what's going on around them. At least make sure you're alone before you start running your mouths in a public restroom for God's sake.

"I'm ok. Let's go." The door slams.

Well, fine. You go shopping and buy your friend some perfume so she can spray it on anything that offends her. Better get the jumbo-sized bottle.

You both probably came through the line, and we shook hands, and you said "sorry" and I smiled to console you.

I pull my pantyhose straight and tight around my waist as I stand. I smooth my dress over my knees and return my feet to their shoes. I push the lever and watch as the water swirls, washing my offenses away. With a soft slide of my finger, the latch on the stall unhooks, and my shoulder guides open the door. Freedom is demanding.

Carl

I walked here to this little dug out grave with everybody else. Followed behind two men balancing the box between them. I stood next to Jack while he threw a hunk of dirt on the smallest casket they make. Bridge wouldn't come out. She stuck her arms across the doorframe and wouldn't let go. Jack left her sitting on the back pew with an old woman in a wheelchair parked next to her.

I listened to the lady sing "I Come to the Garden Alone." I hated it. I shook hands with people I know and don't know—again. I let Rob pat me on the shoulder. I smiled when the preacher said goodbye and offered his blessing. I did most everything I was supposed to, so what's it to anybody if I want to stay out here and have a smoke?

There's nobody to see me unless they want to watch. They're in the hall stuffing their cheeks fat with funeral food. Something about death makes people hungry. They say the food's for the family but it ain't. It's for everybody else. Like eating will keep you alive. Jack and Bridge are the ones needing to eat, 'specially Bridge. When you stop eating, that's when the trouble starts. It's no good after that.

Kate

It's like she's on a campaign or something. Shaking hands and smiling, too much nodding. Get a glass of tea and sit down. Everybody's seen you, Mama.

If I'd been a mother, it would've been all love and lunches. Fun. He'd (I don't know what makes me think it was a boy) wear whatever he wanted to church—if we felt like waking up for it.

I'd make crispy waffles for him on Sundays and strawberry PopTarts the other days. We'd play games in the yard—I'd get a house for us somewhere we could run and play without worrying about flowerbeds. We'd have money for slinkies at Kmart and ice cream cones after. We'd sleep outside even when it was cold. We'd cuddle under a fleece blanket and the breath from our laughter would keep us warm.

When I couldn't stand it anymore—the schedule and schoolwork and sleepless nights—I'd take him to Mom with his overnight bag—a blue one with his initials embroidered on it—bursting at the zipper seams. I'd say I was going grocery shopping and go on and on about how it'd be easier without him pestering me beside the cart grabbing at this thing and that and how I needed to go the bank too and could she watch him until I was done and I'd be right back as soon as I was through.

I'd kiss him and squeeze him tight so Mama might take a second look. A look she'd remember months down the road as the moment she knew I was never coming back.

When people saw him at church or climbing down the school bus steps, they'd say, "What a shame" and shake their heads. They'd ask across their kitchen tables, "How could she leave him?" and when he grew older they might say, "He looks a little like his mother."

Mama would get all the credit. If he did well in school, it'd be because "Virginia makes sure he does all his homework." If someone said he was handsome it'd be because "Virginia presses his clothes and combs his hair."

She'd keep her title for being a saint. This would guarantee a crown. By the time everyone had a say, I'd never have existed.

Virginia

Bridge and Jack left—just as well. Kate and Rob leaning against two opposite walls like brooms. Carl nowhere to be found. Typical.

A little bit of coffee cemented to the pot. A few chicken salad triangles and one or two spoonfuls of potato salad remain. No matter. All the platters and bowls even the burnt coffee will be empty soon. People love free food on all occasions.

Vera's still here. Propping her ugly sun hat with one finger every chance she gets—for attention. No one wears hats anymore.

"Oh, Virginia," she says. "You look exhausted. Have you tried a slice of my cake yet? One little bite will perk you right up." She shoves a sagging paper plate in my face with frosting dripping over the side.

"I'm all right. Thank you though."

"I cracked and flaked the coconut myself. None of those store-bought flakes everybody uses nowadays."

"No thank you." I step back.

"Just a smidge." She pushes it forward, the plate's edge near my nose. "You'll thank me."

All I meant to do was move her hand aside, get the sickening, too-sweet smell away, but it hit the floor. Cake side down. Frosting smashed and leaking underneath the overturned plate.

"Vera," I say. "I'm so sorry. I didn't mean for that to happen."

There is no reply—only a look of doubt and disgust as she darts past the buffet table.

I turn the plate right side up and use its edge to scoop what I can. The frosting is thick and unforgiving, pasting itself to the linoleum with each swipe of the napkins somebody dropped beside me.

I wave away all offers of help. This is my mess to clean up, but I'll need cleanser and paper towels.

In the kitchen, Vera strangles a wet rag over the sink. The two ladies who'd cared for the buffet earlier stand on either side of her, nodding.

"And I didn't actually see the child of course, but I have this friend who knows. This sort of thing happens more to those types, you know—the ones with head problems," Vera says, pointing to her temple. "All I wanted to do was make something nice, and she goes and does this on purpose. Takes hours to make you know. You'd think they'd all be more appreciative, considering." She dabs the rag under one eye then the other. One of the ladies pats her on the shoulder.

"Head problems? Considering what?" I march through the doorway like a soldier, head up, shoulders back. "Nobody here gives one good Goddamn—Lord, forgive me—about your cake. Everybody knows all you do is run your mouth about everybody else. And the ones that don't know will soon enough." I glare at each woman then return my stare to Vera. "You've talked about who's too fat and who got too skinny trying not to be so fat. You talked about Rose Cox stealing prescription medication from her grandmother. How would you know? Were you there? Now you're back to us."

I jerk the paper towel roll from its hook, and grab the bottle of Pine-Sol, leaving the cabinet door to slam shut.

"You think you know everything about me?" Vera chases me, shouting, as we reenter the fellowship hall. "There's been many a time when you had a listening ear in one or two of my conversations. Well, let me tell you something else you don't know 'cause if you did, you wouldn't be walking around so high and mighty." She grabs my arm, spinning me toward her.

"When Kate was in high school I saw her coming out of that women's clinic in Roanoke. That's right. The one where they do the you-know-whats. I was driving downtown trying to find a music store that sold this certain kind of guitar strings Paul Jr. wanted, and there she was walking out the door in a grey Appalachian State sweatshirt. I didn't know for sure it was her until just the other day when I saw her wearing the same one over her grocery apron."

My face, arms, hands, legs all flash with heat. I'm burning to death.

I look at Kate. She's still. Her eyes give her away every time. My God.

Rob

When Kate was little, I'd lift her to up to reach Daddy's red cap off the nail. Mama left it hanging over the March 1980 calendar page, the year he died. He'd smoked like a chimney—on the tractor, feeding the hogs, between bites of meatloaf on Sundays, so it was the kind of surprise you expect when the doctor told him "six months at the most."

She'd smile and tug at my pants leg, never taking her eyes off the old cap. She'd pull at it, but it'd always get stuck on the nail head, so I'd help her the rest of the way. She'd work it on her little brown head, and the brim would fall down over her eyes. When she'd look up at me, all I could see was her nose and lips. I'd laugh, and she'd start. We'd stay that way—me standing there holding her, loving each other like that until she got tired of the game and wriggled down. I'd grab the cap before she ran off and tuck it back on the nail for next time.

One time, I cried. The sobbing kind with a mind of its own that has to run its course. Something about the calendar and days passing and Daddy gone—I don't know. I couldn't help it. Her little almond eyes opened wider and wider as she focused on my face and her bottom lip trembled. I thought for a minute her own tears might come, but they never did. My shoulders heaved as I held her—maybe that was what scared her.

The shocked, embarrassed, sad little face—larger eyes and a deeper quiver in the chin now—is the same. Don't turn it toward me, please.

Kate

I slam the car door and grind the engine to a start. "Fuck" I yell out loud and slam both hands on the steering wheel. What am I supposed to do now? Mrs. Bern, the old crow. She's done it now. The look on Mama's face—embarrassed to death. Hell, she'll probably move. And Daddy, standing there looking at the floor. What did I expect? Them to say something to her? Stand up for me? Come running after me? Right.

I'll have to leave. I can't go home. Not to Mama and her "How could you do this to me?" or Daddy and his silence. I don't know which one is worse.

Go somewhere else. Get out of here and into a real life where everybody you know isn't tracking your every move. People have lives of their own somewhere, and they live them and let you live yours.

I dig in the glove box for a pack of old cigarettes I keep in case of emergency. Two left. I light one, inhale deep, then force the smoke through my nose. What the Hell—it feels better.

I can either go home and grab my stuff now before Mama gets there or go by the trailer park first. I mean the least I can do is tell her bye, considering.

I put the car in drive and barrel through the parking lot. The brakes squeal at the bottom of the hill. I look left, glance right, and turn.

Jack

"Bridge, you asleep?" I call to her. She doesn't answer. I lean my head to the side, thinking I might go back there, crack the door open a little, just enough for me to see her. I don't though. I don't know why—maybe because I'd like for her to be the one checking on me.

She's been in the bedroom since we got home. I tried to get her to eat a peanut butter sandwich when we got back since we didn't eat a bite after the service. She pulled at the sleeve on my coat as we walked to the fellowship hall, whispering "home" over and over, so I figured we'd better not stay long. I did get a glimpse at all the food laid out on the tables, and it all looked good.

I helped her get her clothes off. I even hung up her dress in the closet. I slipped her nightgown over her head while she held her arms up for me. Anybody looking on right then might not think a thing was wrong in our lives. I pulled the bedcovers back for her and she slid right in. Her eyes were already closed, but I believe she whispered "thank you."

No need for me to stay in dress clothes either, so I hang mine over the chair. Only some family might stop by later, if that. I'll be fine in an old pair of blue jeans, the soft kind it takes years to break in, and a cutoff t-shirt. Some guys call them "wife-beaters," but I never have.

I pop the cap off a bottle of beer. A few boys from work brought me a 6-pack of imported beer. I'll take a couple more outside.

I take a swallow, sit the bottle on the porch, and rest the back of my head on the chair. I've no more shut my eyes when I hear the crunch of gravel. Kate's grey Topaz is chewing and spitting rocks as she barrels up the road. She flings a still-smoking cigarette butt out her window as she slams on the brakes.

Two visits in three days. So this is what it takes to bring sisters together.

Virginia

Rob is on the front porch. He'd said it smelled like rain. He was watching the lightning bugs just starting to come out. He'd quit rubbing his fingers over his eyebrows, pulling at them a little as he'd go. When we were together, I'd tell him he wouldn't have any left if he didn't leave them alone. Nerves, I guess.

After everything—Kate running off like she did, and the rest of us leaving, without so much as a word like nothing'd ever happened—he'd offered to come over, see if "I got home all right," "needed anything," and "maybe we should talk." He stammered and stumbled in the parking lot coming up with more and more reasons for a visit. I half-listened to him as I watched a crowd of old crows walk Vera to her car. Like she was the one needing consoling. I had to bury two grandchildren today. People'll turn on you on a dime.

His shoulders jerk at the sound of the screen door as it opens. I bring him the iced tea he'd asked for. It's half-full. Mine is spilling over the top—a little Jack Daniel's in mine.

I knew I'd get home all right, I didn't need anything, and I didn't want to talk or think—not about Kate or Bridge or you. Lord, forgive me for wanting to be alone.

Drink what you have and go home.

He's rambling about my flowerbeds and how moles have torn up his yard. I sink into the rocker, take a long sip, and slip off my shoes.

Cross at the ankles.

Dress for supper.

Ladies always wear a smile.

Mother's sayings flash through my mind.

We'd spent all day cleaning her bedroom. Me and Kate. The two of us getting along for once. Laughing at an old feathered fedora of Daddy's and the picture of me in my tap dance costume.

I was an only child. The only one to change her soiled adult diapers, the only one to wipe mashed potatoes from her chin, the only one to choose her burial dress.

She was imported to Mt. Laurel by the schools. They needed a teacher, and she accepted until I was born. Besides reading and math, she taught little girls how to be grown up ladies and little boys how to be grown up gentlemen. She carried those lessons home. Pressed linen tablecloths and napkins that were never supposed to touch so much as a biscuit crumb, lights on before seven and out before nine so neighbors wouldn't think of us as lazy or night owls. Etiquette classes for me an hour away every Saturday, and a suit and tie at all Rotary Club meetings for Daddy—even the pancake breakfasts. We didn't complain. Me and daddy. At least not to each other.

When he died at forty-two, Mother folded our grief into everyday life. In full makeup and hard-sprayed hair, she answered every house call with an appropriate smile. She invited each visitor in for coffee and cake as she marveled over their offerings of pie and sandwiches. They all shared the same look of surprise and contempt at her cheerfulness as they declined.

Kate was somewhere—I think loading the boxes to be taken to the Salvation Army, and I picked up mother's jewelry box. Under an empty velvet ring box was a piece of paper folded into a small square. A love letter from Daddy.

> *April 10, 1960*
> *Dear Evelyn,*
> *I am a new man because of time spent with you. Your laugh,*
> *your touch, the scent of your hair—all of you, I love.*
> *I will leave them for you if you ask me to. I will.*
> *Forever yours,*
> *David*

My mother's name was Florence.

Bridge

Jesus loves the little children. All the children of the world. We are precious in his sight.

I saw you looking but trying not to look. At the balloon—popped without the party, the sagging, hanging skin around *our* belly—my belly. I'm the only child left.

Kate

"Can I get one of those?" I stare at the beer, praying there's some left.

"In the fridge. This kind here is a little strong," Jack says. "You might like it."

I walk inside, grab a bottle, and head back out. I need a drink first. A little something to calm me, my nerves, my mind, whatever.

"You got a—"

He hands me an opener. Jasper's Tire and Auto is printed on the handle.

He doesn't bother looking at me when I sit on the step, my back to him, instead of in the other chair. One good thing about Jack is he doesn't judge. At least not to my face. He's not a talker either, which is good, and he doesn't mind silence, which is better. We've spent more than a few hours sitting on porches drinking beers not saying a word. The family get-togethers when everybody is inside catching up on who did what to who and when, there we'd be—outside, together, but by ourselves. The one thing we have in common is nobody's much interested in catching up with us.

"Bridge awake?" I break the silence, the rules, but I have to. I don't have much time.

"Don't know."

I stand, drain the last sip of beer, and pick up his empty bottle. He never opened his eyes.

"Need to see her just a minute before I go." I don't know why I'm telling him this.

He grunts. Eyes still closed. Hell, I think he's asleep.

I toss the empty bottles in the trashcan under the sink. If she was sleeping before, she's not now.

"Bridge," I say. I push open the door and move to her side of the bed.

She sits up, resting her back against the headboard.

"Were you asleep?"

No answer.

"You need anything?"

"Like what?"

"I don't know. A drink or something," I say. "You want me to turn on the TV?"

"The fan."

I walk to the chest of drawers and turn the knob.

"High," she says. I press the button to circulate, too.

"I'm think I'm heading out for a while," I say. I stay next to the chest of drawers instead of moving back to Bridge's side. It feels good here. The air feels good. Not cold but cleansing this stale room somehow.

Bridge slides her legs from under the covers and sits on the side of the bed. She opens the drawer on her nightstand and pulls out GiGi's jewelry box.

She waves a hundred dollar bill in the air.

I step toward her, but my foot snags a folded corner of the throw rug, and I yank at the bedcovers trying to catch myself on the way down.

Bridge lets out a holler of a laugh. One I haven't heard since forever.

"Funny," I say. I smile as I straighten my dress and the rug and take a seat on the floor in front of her.

"Here," she says.

I don't have a pocket. I shove the money under my bra strap. "You sure?"

She nods and lifts the jewelry box from the table and sits it in her lap. She flips through a few black and white squares, one over the other, slow and real gentle, before handing one to me.

Mama took Polaroids.

It's a picture of me when I was holding the baby. Me looking down at her perfect shiny black hair—*ebony* is the word fairy-tales use. Skin as white as snow. Lips as red as blood. Like she might wake up if someone kissed her. Snow White was always Bridge's favorite.

I give Bridge the picture back and focus on her feet. Purple vein maps run across the tops.

She wiggles her toes.

I wrap my hands around her heels, bury my face between her feet, and cry.

Carl

I don't know what the hell went on. They're all crazy. That's why I never took to going to church with Pauline. Seems like most of the people shouting how much they love Jesus are the same ones treating you like a dog. I think half the time she just went to keep the peace with her mama, and the other half was to try to get Jack on a good path. She did spend most of her life doing for others. I know how much she did for me.

I was rubbing my smoke out on the sole of my shoe when I seen Kate come running out. Slammed herself in the car and took off like a shot.

Then more people came pouring out the door. A pack of women helped Vera Bern to her car. I all but got run over trying to walk back inside. Virginia was flitting about the hall like a chicken with her head cut off, thanking folks for coming even as they pushed past.

Rob took off after Virginia, and there I stood with the leftover food. One of the plastic dishes didn't have no name on the bottom, so I stuck the sandwiches and potato salad and two sweet pickles in it and left.

Mt. Laurel

Did you see the look on Virginia's face? And Rob? He stood there like a lump on stump.

At least Bridge and Jack had left.

Rob and Virginia have had nothing but trouble with both of them— pretty girls, though.

Food could've been better. Wasn't much selection.

Poor Vera. Had no choice after Virginia lashed out at her like she did.

Bridget and Jack didn't even bother staying. Looks like they'd at least told people they were leaving after all we've done.

Good thing Virginia let it go—Vera's crazy as a June bug.

Didn't I tell you Kate was the type? Flitting from one to the next. Caught up with her.

Need to keep all of them in our prayers.

Better than the soap operas.

Where'd Carl run off to?

The roses in one of the arrangements were wilted. You see 'em?

Virginia was dressed to the nines as usual. That woman don't miss a beat.

I was hoping to see the little dear.

Kate

Stayed longer at Bridge's than I meant to. We haven't spent that much time together since we were kids. I crawled up in the bed with her and watched television. I thought maybe I should tell her what happened—maybe she had a right to know. It was her daughter's funeral and all, but it didn't seem like the right time. She wasn't talking or laughing or anything, but she seemed a little different. There was a heaviness gone from her face or something. I don't know. Maybe I'm the one that's crazy.

The sun's almost set when I pull into the car wash. I don't know why I'm doing this now, but Mama's home by now, and I didn't get my stuff, and I don't know where else to go.

I find three quarters in the cup holder and chunk two in the slot. The sprayer fills with water, and I lift it from its holster and point it at the roof. Always start at the top.

When I was little, Daddy took me to the car wash with him two Saturdays a month. Our town never had one of the fancy ones where you can stay in the car and take a ride through a washing tunnel. The one we had took fifty cents (still does). For that, you got four minutes of rinse, soap, and wax (though we never used it) gushing from a sprayer that left your hand tingling after you were done.

He never let me out of the car. He never told me why. Probably a combination of not wanting me to get wet and not ask him questions while he was working. He never did like me or Bridge asking him questions. He either said nothing or "I don't know" to all of them. I still liked going with him, though—the purple soap suds drizzling down the windshield, the buzz of the high voltage water rinsing us clean, when we broke the speed limit driving home drying the car.

The buzzer goes off telling me I have thirty seconds left to rinse. I make my way around one last time, lifting the long black rubber hose as I go so it doesn't bang against the car. I like to end where I started—the driver's side door. I guess because that's what Daddy used to do. It's near the control box, too, so you get all the time you can for the money.

I take the extra quarter from my pocket and sit it on top of the box for somebody to find if they need it. Daddy did that too.

Rob

"Goodnight," Virginia says. She gets up from the rocker, walks inside, and turns the porch light off. That's her way. I'd come to talk. Offered to discuss things like she said we never did, and now she didn't want to. She just pitched the rocker forward and back, taking small sips at first, then large swallows of her tea—mixed with some sort of liquor I'm sure. She could hide her drinking from everybody but me.

I thought I was a good father to them. I was no Robert Young but good enough. Coached softball and bought cookies for Girl Scout meetings, never shipped them off when Virginia went out of town. I took a drink. Could anyone blame me? I was alone. Who did it hurt? I'd put up with Virginia's on again off again "if nobody notices I'm not really drinking" act for years. Mine didn't last long. It was to make things—all the bad things—go away just for a minute. I knew when it was time to stop.

Things got worse, though, after I left. I'm no dummy, but I didn't know what to say then. "Girls, I'm leaving because your mama's took up with another man." No, I couldn't say that. I couldn't leave them, fourteen and sixteen years old, mad and hurt at their own mama. I thought I was doing them all a favor.

I moved out to the old home place where Virginia refused to live even when Granddaddy offered to build a new house for us on the property. She'd seen the road flood down in the bottom field and wouldn't for one minute, she said, live somewhere she couldn't get out of if she wanted.

Bridge and Kate came to visit. Three Saturdays a month, then two, then Bridge stopped coming. More of her troubles, I guess. Then in and out of hospitals and all. Around the same time Kate stopped coming.

We'd been split about a year when I was outside raking leaves, and Virginia come barreling up the driveway and jumped out of the car.

"What the Hell are you doing?" she asked.

"Raking."

"About your daughters, I mean." She slammed her car door.

"What do you want me to do?" I never looked up, just kept on adding to the pile.

"Pay them some attention. Come pick Kate up. Take her to get ice cream. Rent a movie. Go visit Bridge. She's there another week."

"Kate doesn't like coming out here, and Bridge needs her rest."

"These girls are almost grown. Kate's talking to boys now. She's got a part-time job. I'm working, and I can't do everything," she said.

"There's nothing I can do when I'm not there."

"You left on your own. That was your decision."

"You never asked me to stay," I said.

Virginia blinked hard, and I could tell she was grinding her back teeth. She did that when she was really angry or didn't know what to say.

Then she got in her car and left, and I didn't see her again until the day Bridge got married. Somehow, even in little Mt. Laurel, something kept us apart. I thought for sure, by now, she'd have served me with divorce papers, but who knows? In her mind, she's probably keeping her mother's commandment that true ladies don't get divorced no matter what. She was a piece of work. The most intimidating woman I ever met. She ran her household. Even planned our wedding from top to bottom without one peep from Virginia. She's half the reason Virginia's the way she is. The other half she probably got from her father truth be told.

Jack

He won't ever get rid of that old pickup. Bet he still keeps Mama's red leather change purse in the glove box.

He's been pretty good through all this though. Surprises me. Didn't have two words to say when Mama died.

"You all right?" he asks, walking up the steps.

"Fine. Needed some fresh air."

"I brought y'all some food. He hands me a small container with a paper napkin and plastic fork balancing on the lid. "Just a little that was leftover from the lunch."

I take a big bite of potato salad and shovel in a sandwich.

"You hear about what all went on?" He takes a seat in the chair next to me.

"Where at?"

"You mean Virginia hadn't been over here? She hasn't called?"

"I took the phone off the hook when we got home so Bridge could get some rest."

"I don't know exactly what, but after y'all left something happened in the fellowship hall. People was tripping over themselves to get out of there, and Mrs. Bern had to be walked to her car."

"Never can tell." I keep chewing.

"That's the truth."

I offer him the last sandwich.

"You go ahead and eat it. I believe I will have one of those pickles though."

"Nice little service."

"Yeah."

"Bridge doing all right?"

"I just checked on her. She's asleep."

"You all right?" He pitches himself back in the rocker and looks up.

"Fine."

"I been thinking about your mama. You?"

"Little bit." I brush the breadcrumbs from my lap, crumple the napkin and toss it next to the empty beer bottles beside my chair.

"Tell you something funny," he says as he shifts his body forward, planting the soles of his feet flat on the porch.

I turn my head just enough to see his back is straight as a board.

"I only have the one suit coat, you know? I put it on this morning when I was getting ready, and I slid my hand in the pocket. Know what was in there?"

Probably a flask. But I didn't say it.

"It was your mama's program from her service. Remember? It had the Jesus picture on the back—the one she liked where he was holding the lamb and all those children were at his feet."

"Yeah," I say. I lied.

"Well, I didn't open it. I folded it in half and put it back in my pocket. Then I took the coat off and hung it in the closet. Don't know the reason, but I just couldn't bring myself to leave the house with that coat. Foolish old man I guess."

"You're not so old," I say. He grins.

"You going back to work tomorrow?" he asks. I'm glad.

"I'm goin' try. Need to have somebody come sit with Bridge though."

"I can do that."

"I'll let you know." I think I need to be the one here with her. I don't know. I need to get back to work too. What if she wakes up and I'm not here? What if it doesn't matter to her?

"All right. Well, I guess I'll go on home." He stands and takes a step toward me. "I'm pretty beat. Expect you need some rest too." He pats me on the knee. That has always been our version of a hug.

I walk him to his truck. It's not far and the porch light is on so he can see, but it feels like the right thing to do.

"Glad you came by," I say. I'm out of breath—partly from the beers and partly from being worn out.

"Sure thing."

"Daddy," I say. He stares at me, hard. His eyes wide and questioning. He's surprised. Me too. I don't think I've called him that to his face in ten years.

I cross my arms and lean into his side mirror. "I don't think I'm doin' right for Bridge. Don't know the right thing to say."

He turns the key and the motor roars—as much as it can for twenty years old. He rests his hand on the steering wheel, his eyes focused on the windshield.

"Nobody does, son. We move beside and around and in between each other until something—sometimes good, mostly bad—pushes us together. Then we have to get close, real close, and it's no easy job for any of us."

Virginia

The ceiling fan raises goose bumps on my arms. My legs are tucked far down under the covers, under the summer quilt stitched together square by square by great-grandmother Eileen. Mother could sew—no, she embroidered. There's a difference. She told me so. She stitched an angel's harp on the layette sets she bought for Bridge and Kate.

I know why she didn't tell me. I won't lay in this bed another minute pretending we're something we're not. We never were. She never liked spending time with me like she did Rob. I was working and I got tired, and the truth is I wanted some time to myself for myself. Time to read a romance novel if I wanted to or watch television at night. I was the room mother for two years in row when she was in elementary school for goodness sake. I chaperoned her class trip in the fifth grade. I laid cool washcloths on hot foreheads. I am not a bad mother. There are just mothers. Even the one down in South Carolina who drowned her kids in the backseat of the car—ran it off into a lake or something—had to have some good in her sometime. She might've given those kids baths at night and washed their hair and combed it and buried her face in it and said, "You smell so good." Or nibbled on their earlobe when she was holding them because her insides were filling with love and pride and worship so that if you didn't bite them right then, you'd explode. Even if she did what she did, at one time, even if it was only for one minute, they felt a mother's love.

I'd run away. They took from me and pulled on me, so sometimes I had to take off. When Mother told me to stop coming to her house because "What would people think?" I ran to Dave. When he was emptied, I ran to the television. I never thought to run to Rob. He was taking from me, too.

His parents were the talk of Mt. Laurel. The Evans family were good people. Everybody said so. That's why Mother didn't mind when I married him—a farmer, hogs no less. A little bit of family money didn't hurt either. Rob was the ticket out of my house. After the honeymoon, he enlisted in the National Guard but never went to Vietnam, which would've made things more exciting.

I hurt him, sure and plenty, over the years. He hurt me, too. He never changed for me, and he never fought for me—that's what hurt most. When he asked me about Dave, and I told him the truth, he didn't cry or look sad or anything. He packed two suitcases, waited till the girls got off the school bus, kissed them, and left.

It was all so much easier with Bridge. I don't know why. Maybe it's because she was gone so much. It's not like we're more alike. Lord knows, neither of my girls are much like me. Good for them, I suppose.

Kate was, *is*, harder. She's tougher, unforgiving almost. She hates everything I always thought was important—a tended garden, smart clothes, agreeableness. After today, the last one is shot to Hell.

Naturally beautiful, really. Soft brown hair with a little wave—just enough to be flattering around the face. My hair is a yellow curly mess always in need of taming.

Coffee-colored eyes and clear skin. I fight acne flare-ups even now.

I stay on her to try because she could be stunning. Have anything she wants. Go anywhere she wants. Looks can get you through the door, make people take you seriously, then you show them what you can do. She defies me on purpose, I'm sure.

We never talked about anything important. I couldn't have told my mother about something like that either. What could I have done to help her? Anything? I couldn't raise another child. And it would've been me, make no mistake. What would Mt. Laurel have to say? The whispers and stares and condescending smiles. Relentless "I don't know how you do its" and an appreciative grin paralyzing my face throughout the day.

I'm sorry for her. I am. God only knows her hurt, Bridge's hurt, mine. I hate to think it, and Lord forgive me, but she did me a favor—keeping it from me.

Now I know. Now I have to *do* something. What now?

Rob

Most everybody's lights are off. The baths and prayers and last drinks of water are done. All of them tucked in, where I should be, but I'm taking the long way home—the back way, over the winding roads, past old houses and abandoned tobacco barns.

Lord knows I tried with her. There were some good times—trips to the Eden drive-in and picnics after church. She jumped at the chance to marry me. And then the girls came along. It wasn't enough for her. I wasn't enough for her. Enough laughs. Enough "I love yous." Enough everything.

"I don't want to get in your business," he'd said, "but I swear I seen Virginia at the ol' motel off 58. Seen her three or four times last month when I was filling the machines. Didn't see you there though."

I can't remember his name—Jimmy, Jeff, something like that. Went through school together, too. Always good at music. Played the trombone in the marching band I think. He went to work filling crackers and soft drinks in vending machines for his uncle.

I was pumping gas, and he'd pulled in next to me. He'd started by asking me how the girls were and work at the furniture factory since Daddy's farm had been sold. "Sorry to hear about your old man," he'd said.

I told him Virginia was fine when he asked even though she wasn't. She'd been mad as a hornet most nights after work and took off to her mama's or locked herself in our bedroom watching the television.

"I know all about that," I'd said. I kept right on squeezing the trigger till the tank was full like I was calm and didn't want to fly right out of there. "Meeting out of town clients for the bank."

"Sure, sure." His words came too quick. "Y'all take care." He took off toward the store with his head down.

I didn't bring it up right away. I left it alone a week before I asked her about it. Every day that week I thought, maybe, Virginia would come home in a good mood, be happy, and that would mean everything was all right. It was just a phase she was going through—trouble at work, worried about Bridge being back and not knowing if she was better this time, another fight with Kate about clothes. Or she'd come right out and tell me about it. It was another man, but it didn't mean anything. She was just upset about all those other things at home. She was sorry, she loved me, and wiping tears from her eyes, she'd say, "Forgive me."

The week went by. I even gave her an extra day. It didn't matter. I knew she was never going to say anything, and I couldn't stand it anymore. I was rinsing the coffee pot. She was walking toward the door.

"Anything you want to tell me?" I didn't look at her. I kept swirling water around in the pot.

"Like what?"

"Rocky Bridge." I jerked the dishtowel off the cabinet knob.

"Oh, that." Her voice was steady. She sat her purse on the counter and took a seat at the kitchen table.

What all happened next was like something out of a movie but not any kind of a movie I'd ever seen. She told me all about it. Everything. How she met him at the bank and it'd been her that started things up, how he was younger which helped her feel younger, too, and how sad and lonely she'd been lately. The whole *affair*, the word she used like she was talking about a party, was over. She'd broken it off because—with me, the girls, and work—it was just getting to be too much.

I don't think I said a word. I must've looked like an idiot standing there rubbing the towel on the coffee pot over and over. She talked at me not to me, like you would a stranger, someone you just met and were talking to about the weather.

She sat there staring at me while I put the coffee pot back on the burner, folded the dishtowel and draped it over the sink. She looked up at me and smiled, actually smiled, as I walked past her toward our bedroom.

I don't know what she did all day, but I never heard the door open until the girls got home from school.

I never knew anyone could be so mean, cause so much hurt and not care.

Kate

God, I hope Mama is asleep. I can't believe I came home, but I'm tired of driving and wearing this dress. She'll want to talk to me tomorrow, get it all out with yelling and gritted teeth. That'll be fine. Get one decent night's sleep in my own bed before the final blowout and before I head out.

I take off my heels at the door and creep down the hall in bare feet. The floor in my room is mess. I stumble over clothes and underwear and shoes as I make my way to the nightstand. I turn the knob on the lamp. *Click. Click.* Great. The light bulb is blown. I climb on my bed to reach the blinds and draw them up. Some moonlight comes through, but the headboard is too wide to let much of it in.

I take off my dress and throw it in the hamper. It's wet and grimy from the car wash. Maybe Mama will still wash for me even if I do leave.

I toss in the bed, rolling over and under the sheet and blanket. Two babies and then not. Two mamas and then not. Two sisters. Two daughters. The scars on the inside of her wrists when she handed me the money. The burn in my throat from the cigarette smoke. The pictures and the handshakes and the eyes—all on us like circus performers. Me on the trapeze, hoping someone will catch me if I can't catch myself.

Thinking and sleeping and fighting both until I can't take it anymore and slide out of bed. I think of when I was little, and I'd have a nightmare, how I'd tiptoe down the hall into Mama and Daddy's room. I'd nudge the door open and get on my hands and knees and crawl so soft and quiet— barely taking a breath as I made my way across the carpet to Mama's side of the bed as not to wake up Daddy. I'd lay on my side, facing her bed, my right hand on the edge of the mattress, waiting. She'd drop her arm over, searching for my hand with her own. Somehow she always knew when I was there.

This time is no different. I edge myself between the throw pillows on the floor. Mama drops her arm over the side, searching for my hand with her own. When she takes hold, my hand in hers, I exhale and close my eyes.

Acknowledgments

The following were previously published, some in slightly different form.

"A Real Woman" excerpted from *Breath to Bones-a Novella*
*This is What America Looks Like: The Washington Writer's
Publishing House Anthology*

"Goodbye Alice."
Appalachian Review

"There Isn't Any More"
r.kv.r.y quarterly

Breath to Bones-a Novella received the Judith Siegel Pearson Award for
Fiction from Wayne State University.

"Sweet Smoke" was shortlisted for the First Annual Coppice Prize from
Redbud.

The author thanks the Converse MFA program for its guidance and
support.

CPSIA information can be obtained
at www.ICGtesting.com
Printed in the USA
LVHW100452170522
718906LV00011B/2045

9 781638 040323